JOE DAVISON

Team Adventure Club

An epic mystery survival story for boys and girls

Second edition

Editing by Karaly Clubb

This book was professionally typeset on Reedsy.
Find out more at reedsy.com

Contents

Preface

Bellevue Heights is a sunny, seaside town that's warm in the afternoon and cool in the evenings. The long stretch of road that runs the length of the town is known as Seaside Drive. It starts some 15 miles at the exit off Interstate 45 and runs south for 25 miles. Along the way you pass towns like Hawks Landing, Fishhook, Eagle Bay—the richest part of Bellevue Heights —and Tropical Estates, which is a series of condos beachside full of retirees...and, of course, Bellevue Heights, established in 1935 by the railroad tycoon, Orbert Schumacher, a German industrialist.

The city of Bellevue Heights was a small, quiet town until World War II. Then it became a booming destination for those who wanted to build a business, buy up land, and build real estate. Its ever-growing population turned into a vacation destination as well, which is how Carrie Calusa's mother and father met back in 2000.

Now, this redheaded 12-year-old is loving it, soaking up the sun, and having the time of her life with her two best friends: Leanne McCallister, a dark-haired daredevil who loves to be upside down as much as right side up, and Robert Whitman, a skinny computer wizard and mechanic. These three can do it all. That's why sometime last summer Carrie announced their new club—Team Adventure Club—which is dedicated to solving mysteries, finding lost animals, and discovering new in faraway places!

They do this with the help of her amazing Uncle Max, a brilliant and often strange goofball. Uncle Max provides special equipment when needed, such as a laser gun or a toothbrush. Uncle Max's story is a long one: once, a long time ago, he helped save the Galaxy in an epic space battle when he was 16 years old. He has been sworn to secrecy by the government. This, however, left the family to believe that he made it all up. Only Team Adventure Club believes him.

Now, let's catch up on this amazing and fantastically crazy group of individuals known as Team Adventure Club!

1

CHAPTER 1

The day started off the same way they always did. Carry and Leanne met in the front of the school, on the steps, while Robbie locked up their custom motorized scooters. Robbie's father, and Leanne's stepfather, is Mr. Whitman of Whitman Insurance, the number one rated insurance company in the city. So, he bought Team Adventure Club the scooters, so they could get around the neighborhood faster. They are awesome. Silver in color, with big fat wheels and a pop-up seat if you want to sit instead of stand while riding. They have a huge headlight on the front, and they have been outfitted with a USB plug for their wrist communication devices, also known as the TAC-COMM.

Robbie finished encoding his custom-designed touch screen lock and hustled his way over to the girls. He looked especially nice with his jeans and blue button down shirt. Carry started to smile at him but quickly frowned when she noticed his interest was focused on Debra Valentine, the school snob. Debra was the popular girl, the one with new clothes all the time and the fanciest shoes money could buy. She walked like she was some kind of English aristocrat, and every morning she arrived to school with an Iced Mocha Frabawhosawhatsit with whipped cream.

Carry and Debra were old enemies. Debra ran the popular kids like she was the queen, and Carry was the smart kid who refused to bow down. Or the nerdy weirdo. Or the book worm. Or any of the other names Debra Valentine has called her.

Carry's eyes narrowed as she watched Robbie smile and wave at Debra. Carry looked at the mathematics book she was holding and politely placed it against the back of Robbie's head. With force. -

Robbie staggered three steps down and looked back at Carry in confusion. "What was that for?" he moaned.

"Why do you drool every time SHE walks by?" Carry asked, pointing a finger.

"What? I don't...um..who?" Robbie tried playing it off as if he wasn't in love with Carry's arch nemesis.

"Robbie, you are gross sometimes." Leanne said with a grunt. "C'mon, Carry, we have to get to class." She grabbed the other girl by her arm and turned her around.

Robbie stood there watching them walk away rubbing his head. "I'm not going to get any smarter if you keep hitting me in the head!" he shouted. "I was trying to pound the knowledge into your skull dummy!" Carry shot him a cheeky grin before heading inside.

Robbie rolled his eyes and followed the girls inside, where they all scattered to their respective classes

Carry found her seat in home room and put her science book on her desk. She loved science and learning how things worked. In fact, she liked most classes — except math. Numbers were the devil. But she managed to eke out a C+ average in algebra, which brings her overall grade down to a B, which she hates. Debra has a B average.

She pulled out her writing pad, which had T.A.C. printed on the top. She flipped it open and looked at her notes before finding her homework. Today was going to be a great day: they were going to dissect a rat. She was giddy with excitement.

Their teacher, Ms. Everborne, walked in pushing a huge cart with several large metal trays each containing a large, dead rat. Carry stretched up in her seat to get a better look. She smiled and looked back at her classmates who all looked a little sick.

Ms. Everborne surveyed the classroom from her spot behind the desk. Her tall stature was intimidating to most students, but Carry thought she was pretty. Her short hair was a shiny silver, and for being what Carry thought was possibly a hundred years old — again not very good with numbers — she was a great teacher.

"Okay, class I'm breaking you into labs today. So, when I call your names come up and get your rodent and supplies, and we will get started." Ms. Everborne said with a huge smile.

Carry waited with barely contained energy to find out who her partner would be. "...next Carry Calusa and Debra Valentine, you are partners. Come get your rodent." Ms. Everborne smiled.

Carry's heart crashed into a thousand pieces, and for a moment her tongue got stuck to the roof of her mouth. Carry and Debra's eyes met from across the room and students heads started to explode in fiery balls of flame. Then Carry leapt up, pulling a giant hammer out of thin air, which she used to squish Debra flat. Then she folded her up, stuck her in an envelope and mailed her to Alaska.

"...Ms. Calusa, come up here please." Ms. Everborne said, pulling Carry out of her imaginary moment of Debra's end.

"Coming!" Carry said, faking a smile and sliding out of her seat. She joined her nemesis at the teacher's desk, trying for an aloof glare. Debra shot a glare of her own back. "I don't like this anymore then you do!" Debra. "I hardly doubt that," Carry snapped back, making sure her fake smile was still firmly in place.

"Well bug brain, we should ace this thing since you're so smart and all." Debra sneered.

Carry motioned to the lab table. "Shall we?" Her smile turned a bit predatory.

Debra looked like she was trying to come up with a way to stuff Carry into her own envelope.

Their mutual fantasy was cut short by Ms. Everborne. "You ladies play nice, or I'll make you permanent partners."

Both girls turned to look at their teacher with wide eyes, mouths falling open in twin looks of shock. But it did get them moving. They walked to one of the available tables that was full of old scars and scratches from previous experiments gone wrong.

Carry unrolled their instruments and laid out the cloth, setting everything up in a nice, neat line. Debra slammed the metal tray on the table, making everything jump — including the pickling liquid the rat was soaking in, getting on Debra's pretty dress. It smelled like old formaldehyde and shoe leather.

"Gross!" Debra squealed. She grabbed one of the brown paper towels sitting on the table and started rubbing hard to get the smell off. She just kept rubbing, but it didn't look like she was making any progress at all. With a small smile, Carry watched her for a moment before picking up the rat to get a closer look.

Debra stopped scrubbing to gasp loudly and stepped back from the table. "What is wrong with you Carry? That is so gross!"

"It's just a dead rat," Carry rolled her eyes. "It's soaked in formaldehyde and is harmless. Besides, we're about to dissect it and find out if it's pregnant or not. This is science!"

Debra slowly stepped back to the table looking like she wanted to be anywhere but in class today. But since she didn't want Carry Calusa to come out looking better than her she swallowed hard and reached out, taking the rat from Carry's hand. She could feel the cold wet fur sliding in her palm. She squeezed a little harder so she didn't drop it, and she heard a crunch. The rat's head seemed to be looking at her, judging her. Debra quickly put the rat back in the tray and forced herself to smile. "You're not so tough Adventure girl."

"Okay Debra." Carry packed as much sarcasm as she thought she could get away with into the words, mindful of their teacher nearby watching. She really didn't want to get stuck with Debra for the rest of the year.

Carry read the instructions Ms. Everborne had passed around and inserted one of the pins they had been given into each of the rat's feet. Now it looked like it was jumping from excitement. Then she picked up the scalpel and started to cut it open. Debra immediately closed her eyes and backed away.

"I can't Ms. Everborne! This is too gross!" Debra screeched. The entire class looked at her. "I mean it's not right. That animal deserves a peaceful rest. And here we are cutting it open."

Ms. Everborne looked up from her desk and stared for a moment. Then smirked. She loved being right about her students; that's why she put her with Carry. She knew Debra would have a hard time this assignment. "Ms.

Valentine, get back to your table and help Ms. Calusa with the project, or I will flunk you both."

"Well, no Ms. Everborne, but this is so gross." Debra looked back at Carry and the rat.

"It's not gross; it's science." Ms. Everborne got up and came to their table. "Here, I'll help." She pulled up a stool and sat down, taking the scalpel from Carry.

"Ms. Everborne, I can do this just fine," Carry whined.

"Of course you can, but you can't do everything yourself. One day you'll find something you can't do so well, and you'll need to ask someone for help. Learning to work as a team is as important as learning to do things for yourself." Ms. Everborne gave her a warm smile.

Carry sighed and nodded, stepping back to watch. "Okay class, everyone gather around this table, and I'll explain everything as I go." With that, Ms. Everborne started dissecting the rat.

There was a low "ewwww" that fell across the class room, but Carry just smiled.

2

CHAPTER 2

Robbie was sitting in class taking notes with glee. He loved history, especially American History. The West. The Civil War. The Steam Age. He loved it all, and his teacher, Mr. Polsty, had the perfect history teacher look. A full beard with no hair on his head, pants stained with yellow chalk around the pockets, and a brown corduroy jacket that had elbow patches.

Robbie wanted desperately to own a jacket just like that. He looked them up on eBay once, but they were more than he could scrape up in allowance money. He also admired that Mr. Polsty smoked a pipe. Even though smoking was disgusting, it seemed that when he saw Mr. Polsty outside on break and smoking his pipe he looked like either Leonardo Da Vinci or a steam boat captain. Either way, Robbie wanted to be just like him when he got old.

"That is why Lewis and Clark were able to mark so many areas down and create the majority of the locations on today's maps. Can you imagine traveling the countryside with Indians and your best friend? One of you on land, the other on the river in a canoe. Your trusty dog at your side." Mr. Polsty continued talking about Lewis and Clark, but Robbie slipped into his own world for a moment, thinking about Team Adventure Club exploring unknown planets, conquering monsters and fighting pirates on the seven seas.

He quickly snapped out of it when Mr. Polsty called his name. "Well, Mr. Whitman?"

Robbie stared at the man he admired, his mind blank. "Ummm...What is Montana?" Robbie hazarded a guess based on a quick glance at his notes.

"Indeed!" Mr. Polsty said with hearty gesture.

With a weak smile, Robbie quickly sank back into his seat, wiping his brow. A chubby boy wearing cargo shorts and a striped button down shirt leaned over to whisper to him. "That was quick! Were you thinking about Debbie Valentine again?" he asked with a smile and a wink.

The boy was Malcolm Donaldson, Robbie's friend. The only reason he wasn't part of Team Adventure Club with the rest of them was because his parents don't allow him to stay out past 7:30 on school nights and 8:30 on the weekends. And they always go away on trips over the summer, which is when Team Adventure Club has most of its adventures.

Robbie shook his head, but his smirk said Malcolm thought otherwise. He knew Robbie was fascinated by Debra, and he constantly teased him about it.

As the bell rang, Robbie and Malcolm headed to their next class together, gym. Malcolm hated gym. He couldn't run. He couldn't climb rope. He couldn't play volleyball, basketball or baseball. He could punch the punching bag, however, so that's what he did for the entire class. He and Robbie would take turns punching the bag, but when it came time to climb rope, swim or run Robbie was head of the class. Malcolm might hate gym, but for Robbie it was never long enough.

Coach Twinkle was a large man; he was tall and wide with bulging muscles and a thick mustache. His nose was pointed downward, and his hair was buzzed short. Most students feared him, and Robbie was no exception. "Robert Whitman! Eight minutes and ten seconds on the mile boy! Pick up the pace. And tell your chubby little friend that walking doesn't count as running!" Coach Twinkle's voice bellowed like a bull horn.

Robbie waited for Malcolm as he slowly walked over the finish line, but just as he was about to say good job to his friend, Coach Twinkle stepped in, over shadowing Malcolm like the sun eclipsing the moon.

"Donaldson! By the end of this year I'm gonna have you running like your friend here. I know it's tough being overweight and chubby. I was there once, too, little fella. I was a fat chocoholic. I ate candy and sugar all day. Then one day I saw a war movie. And I knew that was for me. I wanted to be a soldier fighting the good fight! From that moment on I worked hard at becoming a light-weight not an over-weight. Say it with me! A light-weight not an over-weight!"

"A light-weight not an over-weight" Malcolm sighed.

"Good. Now hit the showers. You smell like a cheeseburger!" Coach Twinkle said, smacking Malcolm on the back with enough force to push him a few feet forward.

Robbie and Malcolm took the opportunity to run while they still could. Back in the locker room, they sat on the bench, catching their breath. Malcolm was slumped over and tired, while Robbie got busy changing back into his school shirt.

"So, are going to come over this weekend and join Team Adventure Club or not?" Robbie's voice was muffled as he pulled his shirt over his head.

"I want to, but my parents want to go to our grandparents for dinner on Sunday. So, probably not. I'll never get to be a member of the club!" Malcolm said with a sigh.

"That's not true! I can make you an honorary member. You can be an outside adviser for the club. If there's ever any cases we can't solve, we'll come to you." Robbie popped his head out of his shirt, his hair sticking up.

"Really?! Do you mean it?" Malcolm's face lit up.

"Yes, of course I mean it." Robbie said. "C'mon we have to get to math class. I have Carry's homework."

"Is she still having trouble in math?" Malcolm asked.

"Isn't she always?" Robbie said, smacking his friend on the shoulder as they walked out the door.

3

CHAPTER 3

Carry sat in her seat, trying to be patient as she waited for Robbie. She really liked him a lot, but Robbie was too dumb to realize it. He was too busy being obsessed with Debra Valentine. Carry couldn't understand how someone like Robbie could have such a huge crush on a mean girl like her. She wondered what she didn't have that Debra had.

As Robbie walked into class, she sighed to herself. He was handsome, well-groomed and stylish. She looked down at herself; her pants were well worn, as were the awesome hiking boots she loved to wear. Her satchel was beyond worn, held together with duct tape on one of the corners, with other parts having been stitched and re-stitched a million times.

"Hello Carry! You okay?"

She jumped, realizing Robbie was now standing over her desk. "What? Oh I must have been day dreaming."

"Here's your homework. I got question seven and ten wrong on purpose. You're not very good in math remember?" Robbie grinned.

"Yeah, thanks a million Robbie." Carry tried to fight back the wave of sadness. Maybe that was why he didn't like her. Maybe she's a little too stupid in math. Maybe that turns Robbie off. Is Debra smarter in math?

"Carry, are you even listening to me?" Robbie poked her arm.

"What?" Carry blinked at him a few times, trying to get her brain back on track.

"Never mind. We have a meeting at 8:30 tonight at the Tree House. Don't forget." Robbie said.

"The Tree House is in my back yard. How am I going to forget?" She mustered up a smirk.

"Yeah right!" Robbie rolled his eyes, and made his way over to his seat, just as their teacher walked in.

"Okay class take your seats and let's get that homework turned in." Mr. Falvo said. He was a short Japanese man with a bow tie. He had a different one every single day, coordinated by color. Mondays they were always blue, Tuesdays yellow, Wednesday it was red, Thursdays were the green ones, and Fridays were a mystery day where he could wear anything he wanted.

He was a genius and had won a great many awards around the world for his theories in mathematics, and he didn't like when students didn't understand. He felt everyone should have a great understanding of all numbers, and it should be easy. Carry, though, didn't like math. She would rather be in science or history class, or reading up on paleontology. Math was just so hard. Thank goodness for computers and calculators.

Mr. Falvo walked down the aisle collecting everyone's homework. When he reached Carry's desk, he examined her paper slowly, occasionally looking at her, nodding his head and squinting his eyes.

"It is quite amazing how much your sevens look just like Robbie Whitman's sevens. Don't you think so Ms. Calusa?"

Carry gave her teacher a wide grin, hoping to come off as unconcerned. "Uh... I guess?"

"Not a guess. Fact. I'm on to you two. That is why I have assigned a special project for you alone, Ms. Calusa." Mr. Falvo's smile made Carry shiver.

He pulled out a workbook with perforated worksheets inside, handing it to her. "This is a study book on basic algebra. You will complete one page per night. There are two-hundred and forty-seven pages of assignments inside. That is two hundred and forty-seven nights of studying simple mathematics."

As Carry felt her eyes beginning to water against her will, her teacher's face softened slightly. "I want you to learn Ms. Calusa. I'm not here to try and trick you into failing. Everyone deserves the chance to succeed. This workbook will help you learn to understand numbers. I'm no different than you — for me, it is spelling. I can solve a quantum equation in a snap, but ask me to spell liverwurst or parameterization, and I'm at a loss. I must spend extra time learning the composition of words so that I can succeed. Do the workbook, and you will succeed with numbers. The key is to learn to enjoy it. I know you have an A in history, and that is because you love history. Figure out how to love math, and you will find yourself just as successful here."

Carry sighed and nodded. She knew Mr. Falvo meant well. And he was right, his spelling was atrocious. Some of the other teachers could barely make out his post-it notes in the teachers' lounge.

She thumbed the workbook, looking at the little drawings of kids smiling and having a blast doing math. "Kids don't actually jump up and down while doing math," she thought. Then she looked around the room and saw Andre Riessig, a German exchange student, actually jumping up and down by the chalk board as he solved the weekly question.

"Weeeeeeeee!" He was shouting just like a kid who just won a toy at the fair.

Carry shook her head, looking over to Robbie who was staring at her. "What?" She asked.

"You could have gotten us both in trouble." Robbie said in a whisper.

"Why didn't you make my numbers look different than yours?" she whispered back.

"Oh, I'm sorry for doing your homework every day!" he grabbed her pencil and threw it to the back of the room. In retaliation, she smacked the back of his head.

Robbie reached back and grabbed the back of her left knee, starting to tickle her. Carry squirmed in her chair trying not to make a sound, but it was no use. She let out a squeak that sounded like a bird had flown into the room. Mr. Falvo looked around to see where the noise had come from.

"Ms. Calusa. Would you like to share something with the class?" He had raised an eyebrow at her.

"No Mr. Falvo. I had to sneeze." She rubbed her nose dramatically.

"Oh, well then. Bless you." He squinted at her.

"Thank you." Carry hid her face and kicked the back of Robbie's chair.

Mr. Falvo returned to the chalk board and drew several objects. "My three favorite objects: the square, the trapezoid and the parallelogram. Can anyone tell me how to find the dimensions of each?" He scanned the sea of raised hands until he found Carry, sitting with her arms firmly folded.

"Ah, Ms. Calusa. Pick one. Just one and come up to the board." He held out a piece of chalk.

Carry looked helplessly at Robbie with wide eyes. After a moment, he reached into his bag. He always carried around a ton of gadgets he was tinkering with for Team Adventure Club. This time, he pulled out a pair of eyeglasses.

"Carry? Don't forget your glasses." He handed them to her.

She paused, cocking her head at him before walking back to take them. "I don't wear glasses," she whispered.

"Just put them on. Trust me."

Carry did as he asked, blinking when the room went to a dull purple color. She pulled them down again, and the room returned to its florescent glory. Put the glasses back on: still purple. Turning back the chalk board, she saw the same drawings waiting for her, and she sighed. Deep down she had hoped they were special magical math answering glasses, but no such luck.

At the chalkboard, she picked the square. As she started to trace it, the glasses activated. To her delight, it traced the square along with her measuring each side and putting the equation right there. 4+5.2+3+6 X 4. Carry wrote the equation on the chalk board, trying to hide that she wanted to be the one jumping up and down for joy this time.

"It's 4s x 4 or 4s to the power of 2." Carry said. "But the measurement is 18.2 because your square is uneven. All the sides are different sizes. So technically it's off but that's the answer I guess."

Mr. Falvo gave her a long look before nodding. "Very good Ms. Calusa. You may have a seat."

As Carry turned to look at him, the glasses started measuring every inch of his body, calculating dimensions, proportions and size. No matter where she looked it did the same. The stapler. The back wall. Sally Johnson's face. The zit on Sally Johnson's' face. The pencil on her desk. The numbers kept coming, piercing her head like pins and needles. She felt dizzy, trying to shake her head to make the numbers stop. She leaned on Mr. Falvo's desk, but when she looked down at her hand it measured that too. She couldn't take anymore, the headache building until she couldn't see straight anymore. As she gave in to the darkness fast approaching, she heard Robbie and Mr. Falvo calling her name, but it was too late. She felt the glasses slide off her face as she hit the ground and everything went dark.

Carry returned to awareness slowly. Blinking open her eyes, the light felt blinding and overwhelming, so she quickly closed them again. She felt around, quickly realizing she was on a table of some sort. Sitting up slowly, she kept her eyes firmly closed. Even then, she could still see the remnants of fractions and equations burned into her eyelids.

Rubbing her eyes, the headache slammed back into her brain. She laid back down again, not wanting to puke, but it was a lost cause. Just as Robbie walked in, everything she had in her stomach came flying out. All over him. Robbie tried moving but as he moved, he slammed into the door bouncing right in the way of Carry's sick, then slipping on it slamming into the floor.

"Robbie?" Carry asked in a weak voice.

"Yes?" Robbie's voice wavered.

"Did I just puke on you?"

"Yes." Carry just sighed.

Nurse Habberdash came into the room armed with paper towels, which she quickly gave to Robbie, who promptly started smearing the puke off his jeans.

"Robbie, you might want to change your clothes sweetie." The nurse said.

He just shot her a dirty look behind her back, then waddled off to the nearby bathroom.

"Carry, I called your parents. Your mother is on her way to pick you up." Nurse Habberdash said. "Have you ever had migraines before?"

"No ma'am." Carry said.

"Well, just lay there until your mother gets here, okay?" The nurse said as she set about cleaning up the puke.

In the bathroom, meanwhile, Robbie was as clean as he could get. Since he didn't regularly come to school with a change of clothes, he was stuck wearing what he had. Getting the puke completely cleaned off was going to be a big problem. Not to mention the smell. He looked in the mirror and saw that he even had puke in his hair, so he washed his face with soap and water as well. But the smell was over whelming.

He stepped out of the bathroom just in time to see Carry's mom, Sandra Calusa, walking away with a still miserable-looking Carry. Sandra Calusa was a tall woman, and she sported the red hair Carry had inherited. Robbie thought she looked like someone from the fifties with the way she dressed, but he knew she was only in her thirties. And she was pretty. He knew that for sure.

"Mrs. Calusa!" Robbie yelled as he ran down the hallway to catch up to them.

Turning, Mrs. Calusa blinked. "Robbie, why are you all wet?"

Carry turned, her eyes still closed. "I puked on him," she whispered.

"Oh my. Robbie, dear, come with us. I'll take you home. You can't spend the rest of the day at school like that." She pulled out her cell phone, already starting to dial. "I'll call your mother and let her know. Take Carry to the car, and I'll check you out."

As she walked away, already chatting with his own mom, Robbie helped Carry out the door and put her in the front seat of the car. He then started rummaging through his bag until he found a sleeping mask. Putting it carefully on Carry, he looked at her closer, concerned. "I'm really sorry Carry. I didn't realize they would make you so sick."

"It's okay Robbie. I'm never cheating again. Not if it causes this much of a headache. Besides it was cool for about thirty seconds. I see potential for the glasses. Once you get out the bugs." She said quietly.

Robbie got in the back seat then snapped his fingers. "Our scooters!" He jumped back out again just as Mrs. Calusa walked up. "Where are you going Robbie? I'm responsible for you!"

"Yes, Mrs. Calusa, I know. But our scooters are here. I'll drive Carry's home, then you can bring me back to get mine." He started running towards the bike rack.

"Fine! But, you've got twenty minutes, and I want you to call me at every corner." She got into the car, giving him a firm look.

Robbie watched as she pulled away then pulled a small monitor out of his bag, connecting it to the scooter. He put his cell phone on its clip and a Bluetooth headset in his ear. He flicked a switch and a light started blinking. Ready, he then started for Carry's house.

Inside the car, Mrs. Calusa looked around as a beeping noise started. "Mom, hit the red switch on the radio." Carry said, already half asleep. She pushed the button, and immediately Robbie started talking.

"Mrs. Calusa, this is Robbie. You're on the tracking monitor radar. All the scooters have them, and they are connected to all the family's vehicles. It's a safety matter. Maximillian rigged them up for us."

"Oh, that's lovely." Mrs. Calusa said as she kept her eyes on the road.

"So, just watch the red dot on your GPS monitor and you can track them at any time." Robbie continued to shout.

"Okay!" Mrs. Calusa shouted back.

"Mother!" Carry cried out, her hands over her ears as she tried to keep her brain from leaking out.

"Oh, I'm sorry dear. Robbie was shouting so I thought maybe I needed to as well." Mrs. Calusa lowered her voice back to a whisper.

"Okay, bye," Robbie shouted.

"Bye Robbie!" Mrs. Calusa shouted back again. "Sorry again dear."

Carry just moaned.

Robbie jetted down the sidewalk and was quickly on the bay side of the city. He could feel the salty ocean air on his skin, which did nothing to drown out the fresh smell of vomit in his clothes. He tried not to breath, but he could only hold his breath for so long. He called to check in with Carry's mom, giving her an update on his progress.

At Carry's house, her mom got her inside and up the stairs to lie down in her own bed. As she waited for Robbie to arrive, she checked the mail, putting a small box addressed to Carry on the table by the front door, then started puttering around the kitchen, pulling out what she would need for dinner later. As she waited, her husband, Theodore Calusa walked in, home a bit early from work.

"Well, hello to the most wonderful woman in the world!" He moved in for a kiss only to be thwarted as Mrs. Calusa didn't notice.

"There's the chicken and sides for dinner tonight. I preheated the oven. Can you be a dear and get that started for me?"

Mr. Calusa just stood there with his lips puckered out making kissy noises.

"I have to take Robbie back to school to get his scooter. Carry puked all over him today." She looked up and finally noticed him, giving him a small kiss with a smile before heading to the master bedroom to change out of her suit.

Mr. Calusa squinted his eyebrows together. "Why did she puke on him?"

"No idea. She got a bad headache and vomited, the nurse said." She called back.

"Is she okay?" Mr. Calusa followed her into the bedroom, concerned.

"She said she's fine but wanted to lay down."

Mr. Calusa headed up the stairs to his daughter's room. "Carry? Sweetie? You okay?"

Carry rolled over on her bed to face the door. "Yeah. I'm fine Dad. My head just hurts a lot."

"What happened?" Mr. Calusa sat down on the edge of her bed, careful not to jostle her.

"I don't know. I was wearing these glasses Robbie made, and they made me sick."

"Oh, gosh sweetie, I'm sorry. Do you want something for the pain?" he asked.

"Mom gave me medicine already. I'll be fine. I have a club meeting tonight so, I have to rest."

"Maybe you should skip the meeting tonight." Mr. Calusa said gently.

Carry snapped the sleeping mask up onto her forehead, looking at her dad through blood shot eyes. She just scanned her father's head as if she was still wearing the glasses. "I've never missed a meeting. Not happening tonight."

"They can have the meeting without you."

"Dad! It's in our back yard. In the tree house. Just like every Wednesday. We have to get ready for this weekend. We have to find Mrs. Keller's dog Pogo, remember?" Carry said.

"Well, you got a few hours until then. Take a nap." He brushed her hair out of her face.

"Ok, dad. Love you." Carry pulled the mask back down over her eyes, laying her head back down.

As he came down the stairs, Robbie came through the door, still in his wet clothes. "So, what happened today at school? Carry told me you made some glasses?"

"Oh, well, yeah. See I took this old glass plate from a calculator and integrated it with a microchip and then added an an instant size algorithm. So when you look at things, it measures and calculates the equations instantly. So you can do things like calculate the distance from one side a cavern to the other in case you have to jump or something. Well, Carry put them on and it made her sick." Robbie shook his head.

" So they still need to be balanced for what and when to measure, I guess," Mr. Calusa said.

"Sure." Robbie assumed he didn't really understand the mechanics of the glasses, so he didn't bother to try and explain further.

"Are you ready Robbie?" Mrs. Calusa popped her head into the room, keys already in hand.

Robbie was more than ready to get his own scooter so he could go home and change into dry, non-smelly clothes. He nodded enthusiastically.

"Okay let's go then. Dear, I put everything in the oven for dinner, just keep an eye on it for me. We'll be back in about twenty minutes. Set the table for five—remember it's Wednesday, so the rest of the club will be here at eight. Don't even try to ask if she's going to miss it." She paused, counting on her fingers for a moment. "Wait. Set it for six. If I know Max, he'll be here too."

Carry laid in bed listening to a local news show on an old brown and yellow radio she had bought at a garage sale last summer. The left dial was missing, and there was sticker of a puppy that seemed to from the 1970s on the top of it. She loved it.

Unfortunately it only got two stations, one that featured a local talk radio show and a second that played a syndicated horror mystery show that aired at 2am. She listened to the news, letting her brain rest after the overload this afternoon, when a news bulletin caught her attention.

"This just in. It appears there is a comet that is going to be flying within the earth's atmosphere just over Bay Side Beach at 11:15 tonight. Scientists speculate that this is a random comet, and there should no cause for alarm. It should crash into the ocean having little effect on anyone or anything. But if you're out at the beach and want to watch something spectacular this should do it."

4

CHAPTER 4

Leanne, oblivious to the trials of her friends, sat in class paying attention to Ms. Yoder explain the universe and talk about space and time. She loved science class. It was her best subject besides math, history and biology. But sitting two rows from her was Debra Valentine.

Debra's face was flawless, and she was so pretty. But, Leanne thought, even though she is pretty she doesn't know how to fly a plane. Leanne had been taking flying lessons for two years now; her father owned MaCalister Air Field and gave lessons for a living, so when Leanne turned ten he started teaching her how to pilot small aircraft.

She could fly a plane on her now, and once, not that her mother knew, she flew her and her dad to the next state to get her mom's favorite dessert from Big Bob's Dessert Den. Mrs. MaCalister still thinks Mr. MaCalister went alone. This made Leanne smile, but reminiscing also made her lose track of the lecture.

Leanne didn't realize she was still staring at Debra until the other girl caught her. "What are you staring at?" she hissed quietly.

"What?" Leanne snapped out of her day dream.

"You were staring at me. Weirdo!"

"I was daydreaming." Leanne apologized.

"Well, maybe you should go see if your girlfriend is okay instead," Debra snapped.

Leanne blinked. "What are you talking about?"

"Oh, you didn't hear that Ms. Adventure herself got sick in math class and threw up all over the nurse station and Robbie Whitman?" Debra looked down her nose as she talked.

"When?"

"Like ten minutes ago." Debra turned her cell phone so Leanne could see a video of Carry passing out. "I'm going to put this up on my blog."

"You better not, Valentine!" Leanne shook her fist at the other girl.

"Or what?" Debra's eyes narrowed dangerously.

"Excuse me. Would you two young ladies prefer to be the ones teaching this class?" Ms. Yoder asked.

Both girls turned back to the front of the room, shaking their heads. Ms. Yoder was an older woman, about fifty or so. Her hair was a wavy mess of salt and pepper color, and she believed that most children were stupid. She was strange, but a good teacher nonetheless. "Well good! Because I would like to continue the lesson for the rest of the class then, if that's okay with either of you?"

"Sorry," Leanne mumbled.

"Sorry," Debra muttered.

"Good. Now if you girls would come up here. I want to demonstrate mass quantum gravitational polarity in the universe." Ms. Yoder said.

Leanne and Debra made their way to the front of the class, both were still embarrassed. Debra quickly covered, waving one hand as if she was in a parade and giving a curtsy to her classmates. She flipped her hair and smiled wide, then winked at everyone. The boys cheered, and Debra's friends clapped.

Leanne just shook her head her head. She looked out over the class and was not impressed. Most only liked Debra so she wouldn't point them out and make fun of them in the hallways. They knew that if you kept your mouth shut and clapped as Debra Valentine walked by, she would leave you alone, but Leanne didn't really understand why everyone was so afraid of her in the first place.

The lesson continued, and when the bell finally rang Leanne had never been happier to get out of that class. She grabbed her bag and ran out of the classroom, pulling out her official T.A.C. Communication wrist-radio to call Carry and find out what was going on.

"Carry what happened in math class? Are you okay?"

Since students weren't allowed to use cell phones unless it was an emergency, Uncle Max had created the devices for the club. They were like a watch, but they had a large face and a camera so everyone could also video chat, record images and take pictures. They called them TAC COM, and they were awesome, to say the least.

"Leanne, hey." Carry's image bleeped on, and Leanne could tell she was in bed.

"What happened?" Leanne repeated.

"It was awful! Robbie made these calculating glasses, but all the numbers hurt my brain." Leanne realized her friend had a mask over her eyes and wasn't moving to take it off.

"Do you still want to have the club meeting tonight?" Leanne asked.

"Yes! I will never miss a meeting, Leanne! What's oath number three?" That Carry was able to scowl through a mask was impressive.

"Oath number three is that members will never miss a Team Adventure Club meeting, no matter what!" Leanne raised her right hand. "I was just checking, grumpy!"

"I know. I'm sorry. My head hurts."

"Okay. I'll be there in a few hours. Where's Robbie?" Leanne asked.

"I think he's home or coming back here. I'm not sure."

"Just get some rest and I'll be there shortly. Leanne, over and out!" She turned her TAC COM off.

Leanne touched the screen, and a small map appeared. Robbie's red dot was moving quickly through the streets, so she knew he had to be on his scooter. She quickly touched the screen again to call him.

"Did you talk to Carry?" Robbie shouted over the noise of his scooter.

"Yeah. What did you do to her?" Leanne asked as she hustled through the halls to her next class.

"I didn't mean too. The glasses started malfunctioning. I have to take them to Uncle Max. He can fix them." She watched him jump his scooter over a ditch. "I'm going home to change. Carry puked all over me."

"You probably deserved it!" The school bell rang loudly.

"Call me later. Get to class before you get a referral."

"Okay. I'll see you guys in a bit." She flipped her TAC COM off and opened the door to her next class. The room was empty. She smacked her forehead, remembering that class was outside today.

She rushed to the window, looking down two stories to the field where the rest of the class was. She pulled out a small device with a hook and a cable on it, and aimed it at the large oak tree several yards away. She fired and attached the other end to the window ledge. A small handle came out of her bag, and she attached it to the cable.

She could see Mrs. Brunswick was turned around talking to another student and wasn't looking in her direction. This was perfect timing, so Leanne hit the release and dropped down by the oak tree. She quickly moved to an open spot with the rest of the class, slinging her backpack off and leaning on it like she had been there forever. Several other students looked at her in amazement.

One in particular, Yogi Zibberaluga, a foreign exchange student, was very impressed.

"Ah, krasavitsa, you are but daring. You and I should be together. No?"

Leanne smiled at him — he wasn't ugly, and his accent was cute. "Well, maybe."

Mrs. Brunswick walked up, doing a double take when she saw Leanne. "Oh, good. We're all here. But Ms. MaCalister shouldn't you be in Economics class? You have art sixth period — this is fifth period sweetie."

Leanne looked around and realized she didn't really know any of the kids in the class except Yogi, who was in her gym class. She groaned. What a day.

5

CHAPTER 5

The large building sat downtown and cast shadows on the other buildings. Its huge glass tower roof beamed the sun's reflections like a satellite bouncing laser signals. There wasn't a spot in the city you couldn't see the tower. "The eye sore of the city," some people called it. "The Hedgestone Tower of Doom," said others. Either way, it was owned by billionaire Sir Oliver Hedgestone. He was an older man, short, and had a slick bald head. He was ruthless and mean, and he had no heirs for his fortune. He was married for a time, but his wife — Susan Elizabeth Marybeth Hedgestone — died of cancer years ago, and he never married again.

The hallways on the top floor were made of marble. The clacking of his expensive shoes rapped on the floor as he walked, six of his assistants hurried to keep up. Sir Oliver Hedgestone never had less than three assistants with him at all times.

A set of large double doors opened, and he made his way into his office. The entire office could see out over Bay Side Beach, Belleview Heights and the entire city. He stepped onto a small carpet, and one of his assistants knelt down and took off his right shoe followed by the left, then slipped his feet into a pair of yellow Crocs.

He continued to his large cherry oak desk, sitting down in his oversized leather chair. Not just leather — Buffalo Leather, with a large buffalo head mounted to the back. He looked down and noticed that his solid gold pen was crooked, so he straightened it, ensuring everything was perfect.

"Well?" He said looking up at his assistants.

They fumbled nervously as all six pulled out notes and paperwork. The first to speak was Jenny Venola, who had been with Sir Oliver Hedgestone the longest.

"I have your stock market ratings. We're up thirty-two percent for today, sir. It seems that endeavor with World Wide Global is paying off. We fired eighteen people today at Hedgestone Coffee, twenty-six people at Hedgestone Power, and we are moving to a completely robotic assembly line at Hedgestone Motors and should see the entire staff of four hundred and eighty released by next Friday. I had H.R. propose a severance package which needs your approval. And you have a meeting with the Governor at 10p.m. for discussion on the recent leak over at Hedgestone Nuclear." She laid a folder on his desk.

He opened a wooden box by pressing a series of numbers on a pad on top. It opened to reveal dark rimmed glasses, which he slid on before reaching for the folder. He looked at the proposal for a moment before leaning back in his chair. "Does this seem reasonable to you Ms. Venola?" He asked.

"Yes. These people will have to feed their families while they look for another job." She adjusted her glasses.

"How long does it take to find a job?"

"It varies, but perhaps at least up to three months or longer sir," she said.

"Proof?"

She held out her hand, and another assistant handed her a piece of paper. "According to the Job and Securities Regulation Association it takes an average person of high school co-dependency three to six months to find a well-paying job. In certain vocations, such as mechanic, baker or construction, it could take up to six months."

"Revamp it! Bring it back to me tomorrow morning."

She picked the folder back up and nodded. She bowed, then waved the assistants out of the office, leaving Sir Oliver Hedgestone alone at his desk. His watched beeped. He looked down at the large gold and silver piece. It was a Tarrant, which were known as the most expensive watches in the world. Each one had a pure ruby in the center, and the rarest — The Aztec Tarrant

— had a piece of Aztec gold. That watch had been missing for years, and Sir Oliver Hedgestone had been taking vacations with a massive exploration team looking for it all over the world.

He went to Africa, Europe, Russia, China, South America and even New Jersey, all with no luck. But he will find it, if it's the last thing he ever does. He looked out over his office and admired his other trophies. Obtained, for the most part, by paying people to take the artifacts from those who found them.

He was constantly on the lookout for the newest and latest discoveries someone had made. Whether it was Roman, Egyptian, Romanian or from Transylvania, he wanted it. Weapons, vases, pots, tools, skulls, tablets — anything and everything he could get.

He leaned back in his chair and tapped his desk. A small drawer opened, and inside was a large remote control. He hit a button, and the large book case started to slide, revealing a 200-inch flat screen television. It had several feeds, all of them playing the news from different parts of the world. He watched for a moment before focusing on the local report. He hit a button, and soon the entire view was of Lucas Fruber, the local news anchor.

"It seems there will be chaos tonight over Bay Side Beach as Ralley's Comet will come completely into our atmosphere and within several miles of the city. There doesn't seem to any real danger as the comet is not large. Once it enters the atmosphere, it will break up into small pieces that will fall into the ocean. So, if you're out by the beach at 11:15p.m. tonight, you should have a great show! Now back to Bob Cotter for the sports."

"This should be a sight." He pulled out his cell phone.

"Sir." A voice said.

"Get me the comet."

"Yes, sir."

6

CHAPTER 6

The dinner table was packed with chicken, potatoes, bread, broccoli and steamed carrots. Mrs. Calusa was pouring the water as Mr. Calusa finished putting the rolls on the table. He leaned over to her and kissed her on her cheek, and she smiled and kissed him back. As they parted, an older man, who was slightly overweight and balding, stood there. He was wearing a black shirt that read "TEAM ADVENTURE CLUB" on the front, and he still had his biker goggles on his forehead. This was Uncle Max.

"Do you have to kiss my sister all the time?" he laughed.

"Trust me it's not all the time," Mr. Calusa said.

"Man, what a night it's going to be! Club meeting. Comet at the beach. It's all so exciting." Uncle Max was loud, and his voice carried. He was constantly excited about everything, and loved Carry, Leanne and Robbie like they were his own children. Robbie walked in, and Uncle Max went nuts.

"Robbie! The Robster!" He made his hands into claws and clacked them in Robbie's direction.

Robbie reached out and high fived him, then they did a fist pound and some sort of hand slap routine that was long and complicated. Then Leanne walked in and Uncle Max went nuts again.

Carry slowly walked down the stairs to join the group, wearing dark sunglasses. Uncle Max looked at her and smiled. "Why the shades, rock star?"

"It's a long story."

Uncle Max dipped down, giving her a hug. " You can tell me over dinner."

They all started to dig in, with Carry explaining what had happened around bites. Robbie filled in the technical bits about what he thought had malfunctioned and how he might be able to fix them. "I'm really impressed Robbie. To be able to put those images on the inside of the glasses is fascinating to say the least. It's almost like a H.U.D." Uncle Max said.

"What's a H.U.D.?" Ms. Calusa asked.

"That means Heads Up Display." Leanne replied for them. "It's so you don't have to look down at the controls — they are projected directly on the glass. Fighter pilots have then on the inside of their helmets now."

"Robbie, you and I can work together and make our own version of TAC HUD sunglasses." Uncle Max started getting excited.

"No!" Carry shouted. "My head still hurts a lot. I can still see a faint outline of everything."

Mr. Calusa took a bite of food, chewing slowly before joining the conversation. "So, you made a pair of eye glasses that calculated the length of an object?"

"Well, yeah. Kind of." Robbie said.

"You kids are fueled by Uncle Max's imagination." Mrs. Calusa shook her head.

"Mom. It's a fact." Carry pointed to her sunglasses.

"Oh, just like that time you guys found that secret portal to the Bermuda Triangle."

"YES!" All four of them shouted.

Mr. Calusa almost choked on his milk. He nodded at his wife that perhaps she should stop.

"Honestly Maximilian, I don't know why you insist on playing these games?" Mrs. Calusa didn't take the hint.

"Sis, I have explained this to you a Maximilian times. We are Team Adventure Club. We seek adventure, fun, excitement, and most of all lost treasure, aliens, monsters and ghosts! Now, I can't do that as a security guard. Well, at least not all the time." He sipped the foam off his root beer.

"Will you ever grow up?" she asked.

"I hope not sis. Where's the fun in that?" Maximilian said as his watched beeped. "7:30 TAC. Let's get these dishes cleaned up so we can get to that club house."

With that, everyone but Mr. and Mrs. Calusa sprang from the table. They had a system worked out. Uncle Max would wash, while Robbie cleared the table, Carry would put the food away, and Leanne dried the dishes. And they worked fast. Their record was ten minutes. It was the only thing Mrs. Calusa loved about the Wednesday night club meeting.

Once the kitchen was spotless, the gang made their way out to the clubhouse. Mrs. Calusa gave them their usual cookie as they headed out. Uncle Max paused in the doorway. "Sandra, why don't you just let the kids have their fun? They're not going to get hurt or anything."

"Max, I know how you were when we were growing up. You made up ridiculous stories about ridiculous things. I just don't want her chasing far-fetched dreams."

"But sis, that's what this world was built on: dreams and far-fetched ideas."

Mrs. Calusa just smiled and shoved her brother out the door.

Carry, Leanne, and Robbie were already in the club house, which sat between two large oak trees. It was huge and even had electricity. Or rather, a long extension cord that ran across the back yard from the garage. Mr. Calusa had ruined four so far because he kept forgetting about them when he mowed the lawn.

Inside there were several bean bag chairs, two office chairs, a dry erase board and an old television with a VCR/DVD combo connected to it. There was also a small digital video camera on a tripod so they could watch surveillance footage of their most recent case. Uncle Max was in charge of hooking it all up.

Carry called the meeting to order, taking attendance and making sure they were all paying attention. " First order of business: Mrs. Keller's three-year-old beagle Pogo is missing for almost two weeks. I'm a little upset at us for having not found Pogo yet."

"I checked all the kennels in town, and both pounds. Pogo is not there." Robbie reported.

"I put Pogo up on the missing dog Facebook page, and no hits yet." Leanne gave her report.

"Did Mrs. Keller have any enemies?" Uncle Max asked.

"Good question. According to her neighbors, her grandson, Richard had visited recently and was upset that he couldn't keep the dog." Carry pointed to the dry erase board where some notes were listed.

"Where does Richard live?" Leanne asked.

"Chucca Valley. Sixty miles from here," Carry used her laser pointer to highlight the city on the large map hanging on the wall.

"We can't go there to check it out until the weekend," Robbie said, dejected.

"I can go during the week," Uncle Max chimed in.

"That might work, Uncle Max. Check out the house. He lives with his parents, Jacky and William Harrison. Oh, and he's nine. So be careful; they're wiry at that age." Carry blinked hard, then suddenly put her head down in her hands and moaned.

"Indeed they are. I'll stay at a distance and only survey." Uncle Max looked at his niece, concerned. "Are you okay, Carry?"

"I still have a wicked headache, and I kind of still see lines and graphs and numbers." she moaned again, then shook herself. "Okay. Moving onto second order of business. There will be a comet tonight at 11:15 just over Bay Side Beach. Who's in?"

"Oh, I'd love to, but I have an economics test on Friday. It's ten percent of my grade this semester. I have to study." Leanne pouted. "And maybe you shouldn't go either with that headache."

"I'm not missing this thing even if my eyes fall out."

The two glared at each other for a moment, but it passed quickly when Robbie jumped in. "I'll go. I'll zip line out to the roof of the shed and meet you in the back alley at 10:25."

"Why so early?" Carry asked.

"We can't take the scooters. I'm not asking if I can go to the beach at that time of night. My parents will bug out like chickens!" Robbie said.

"Good point." Carry nodded.

"I'm all in. Have to verify something for a friend anyways. Make sure this isn't a micro-burst-freezing missile sent here from the planet Ort Ort." Uncle

Max said as his TAC COM beeped. "I could talk to your parents for you if you want."

All three just looked at him. "Or maybe not."

He quickly looked at his TAC COM. On the screen was something strange — it seemed to be yelling at him. He looked up at everyone and quickly put his hand behind his back.

"Should you take that Uncle Max?" Carry asked.

"What? This? No. Not important. They'll call back," he said.

The device stopped beeping, and Uncle Max gave a sigh of relief. Formal part over, the rest of the club members also relaxed.

Carry went to the dry erase board and wrote the week's instructions for finding Mrs. Keller's dog, while Robbie pulled out the equation glasses and handed them to Uncle Max.

"I can't figure out why they went all crazy."

Uncle Max looked at them for a moment, turning them this way and that way. He opened up the arms and tried looking through them without putting them on. He could see that they were still working. Tiny graphs, lines and numbers were bouncing all over the place, measuring everything. Uncle Max took a deep breath. "Well here goes nothing." Everything turned purple for a moment, then he was inundated with information, and no matter what he looked at, it was measured and drawn out.

He could only think of one thing to say. "Wow!"

The glasses didn't faze him like they did Carry. He had seen this kind of craftsmanship before, a long time ago, in a galaxy not so far away. He knew exactly how to control the amount of information he was seeing and when to expect things and when not to. You actually had to look past the glasses if you didn't want to see the information. "Robbie, these are fantastic!"

"Thanks!"

"Why didn't you get sick?" Carry asked

"I've seen things like this before. These are great! Some of the best I've seen, really. This is exactly the kind of stuff we need for Team Adventure Club! I think I can create a way to have a menu on it, and storage, so you can call up just the information you need, when you need it. They'll become a large asset to us once they're done. Great job Robbie!"

7

CHAPTER 7

It was cold outside, so the steam was pouring off of Sir Oliver Hedgestone's head in waves. Jenny stood in her suit, shivering. She held a briefcase in one hand and a coffee in the other, and in the large airplane hangar behind her sat three Lear Jets. Everything said Hedgestone Enterprises in big letters on the sides.

A large Hummer Limo sat idle as they watched a smaller aircraft taxi in. Sir Oliver Hedgestone took his coffee — and the small warmth it provided — from Jenny.

"Doesn't the night air make you feel vibrant?" He didn't expect an answer, and she was smart enough not to give one. "The night just gets into your lungs." He spent several long moments just breathing in the air before taking a sip and handing the coffee cup back.

Sir Oliver Hedgestone watched as the plane grew nearer. He motioned to two large men in black suits standing in the distance to come closer. These were his bodyguards. Louis, his head bodyguard, was ex-military, ex-CIA, ex-FBI and ex-personality. As far as anyone could tell, he had never laughed a day in his life. The other man, Mark, was shorter and spoke with a Texan accent. He was second in command, and he was also ex-everything you could think of.

As they waited, the plane came to a stop, and the door opened. A thin man with a pony tail and a smile as wide as Florida stepped out, coming down the stairs. He was wearing cargo shorts, an open Hawaiian shirt with a tee-shirt underneath, a large necklace with a shark's tooth on it and sandals. Following him was a shorter, heavier man wearing cargo shorts. The two adventurers — Sam and William — didn't technically work for Sir Oliver Hedgestone, but they did go out and find priceless artifacts for him on a regular basis.

William pulled his pony tail back as he moved closer. "Mr. Hedgestone!" He exclaimed.

"It's Sir Hedgestone." Louis' voice was flat and emotionless.

William looked back at his partner, and they both shrugged. "Okay. Sir Mr. Hedgestone." William repeated.

"No. Just Sir. It's a title given by the Queen of England," Jenny stepped in.

Sam and William both shrugged again. "Sir Hedgestone it is!" Sam said holding out a metal briefcase.

Sir Oliver Hedgestone nodded to Louis, who stepped closer and motioned to Sam to open the case. Sir Oliver Hedgestone smiled as the contents inside gleamed out.

"Now, this was a little trickier to get then we had first thought. It was something of a customs issue as well, Mr. Sir. Sir Mr. Hedgestone." William laughed.

"Gentlemen, we agreed on a price regardless of what it cost you to acquire said product. I am only going to pay what we agreed upon." Jenny replied for her employer.

Sir Oliver Hedgestone reached into the case and picked up the large ruby. It was almost the size of his hand. He held it between his thumb and fore finger admiring it for a long moment before returning it to the case and walking away.

"Leave the money. Let's go." The driver quickly opened the limo door as he approached.

Jenny motioned to the men to leave the case. William took the case from Sam and put it on the ground, and only then Jenny slid a second case to them. She picked up the one with the ruby and started to follow her boss. She heard an exchange behind her as the two adventurers took their money and ran, but she didn't pay much attention.

Getting into the limo, she put Sir Oliver Hedgestone's coffee into a drink warmer and watched as Louis and Mark got into a black sedan waiting next to the limo. Jenny put the case next to her on the seat then pulled out her leather legal pad. She began reviewing the items on her list for the day when her watch beeped. "Sir, it's a quarter to eleven. Did you want to try and make it to Bay Side Beach this evening?"

"The night is going splendid. Yes, let's head to the beach and watch a comet fall. If all goes well it will land in the sand, and we will be able to collect that as well."

Jenny nodded. "As you wish, Sir." She tapped on the privacy window and gave the new instructions to the driver.

8

CHAPTER 8

Robbie's TAC COM beeped, and he sprung from bed like a ninja. He was already dressed, and he even had his shoes on. He slung his bag onto his back and moved quickly, snapping his zip line handle into place. The cable ran from his window to a large tree in his yard. His parents let him have it because they couldn't disagree that it was handy in case of a fire or other house emergencies.

Carry was up and playing another round of Pony vs Pony, a popular online game. She had to keep her computer speakers on low so no one could hear the game and its catchy tune. Then her TAC COM beeped. She made her last move in the game and closed it out. She would have to come back later and beat the pants off Speedy Lady Lord another time.

Robbie landed with ease on the soft ground and opened the side door to the garage. He looked at his scooter and knew that was a dead give-away, so he opted for his skateboard. He ran out of the garage and was met by Carry, who was on her bicycle. She was dressed all in black.

Robbie looked at her. "You look awesome!"

Carry smiled. "Thanks!"

"Are you still having headaches?"

"No, they just stopped, thank god," she said, tossing him a tow line. "Let's go!"

"No Leanne huh?" Robbie asked as he made sure he had a good grip on the rope.

"Nope. That's okay though. This isn't officially a Team Adventure Club assignment."

Robbie held on as they set off. His skateboard was slightly different than most; he had two strange canisters on the rear and a pedal on the front, although he wasn't using them at the moment. There was also a hose that went from each of the canisters to another metal canister on the side connected to the pedal electronically.

Carry's bicycle was also slightly different. She had a gas engine she could switch on that could get the bike up to twenty miles an hour. But tonight, she was peddling. It was quieter, and it was easy on the way to the beach — the whole way was downhill.

Leanne sat at her desk looking over her economics book, hating every minute of it. She was falling asleep as she read every word. Then her head jerk as she snapped awake. She had a thin line of drool coming out of her mouth. She wiped it away and rubbed her face. She tapped her keyboard and her screen blinked, then a meteorologist page popped up with a tracker following the comet.

She looked at that, then back at her notebook. She wanted to go to the beach, but if she failed the test on Friday she could only get a "C" in the class. She just couldn't miss this though. Decision made, she slipped out of the house and was on her scooter, speeding her way down the sidewalk with ease in no time flat.

Uncle Max was already at the beach, and he had a telescope set up and linked to his industrial rubber encased laptop. He had a table, with all his monitoring equipment carefully laid out: there was a satellite communications switch board plugged into a miniature satellite array; a printer spitting out readings and signal messages from the National Radio Astronomy Observatory Station in New Mexico; a flat screen monitor with a grid that was tracking the comet and another giving weather reports; he even had a short band radio tuned into a local news station. He was more than set. He used his binoculars to scan the night sky, but there still was no sign of the so-called comet. He changed the settings on the binoculars to read for thermal imaging. Still nothing.

He sat back down in his beach chair and popped open a root beer and pulled out an oatmeal cream pie. He noticed that people were starting to make their way onto the beach. Checking his TAC COM he saw that the team was almost there. All three of them.

Uncle Max started to become antsy as people started to get closer to his table, asking questions. He quickly covered his equipment with a tarp and crawled under it so no one could see him either. His TAC COM alerted him again.

"Uncle Max, where are you?" Robbie's face popped up.

"I'm under a tarp. I'm starting to feel compromised!"

"What you talking about?" Robbie asked.

"There's too many people here now."

"How many?" Robbie asked.

Uncle Max peeked his head out from under the tarp and looked around quickly. "Four or five now."

"Okay, hold tight. We're about two minutes away."

"I know. I have you on monitor," Uncle Max said.

"Over and out!"

Meanwhile, Leanne was breezing down the boardwalk. She made it to the beach and found Uncle Max's combat SUV and his makeshift tent, but she didn't see Carry or Robbie's scooters. She made her way down the ramp to the beach until the scooter starting having trouble in the deep sand. She parked it at the nearest bike rack and locked it down.

Before she had a chance to start for the tarp tent, Carry popped out from behind the SUV. "About time!"

Leanne jumped and hugged her friend. They walked arm-in-arm to where the boys were waiting, and Leanne got a full view of Uncle Max's set up. Robbie had convinced him to put aluminum poles up, holding one side of the tarp over the table full of consoles and satellites.

Uncle Max sat in his chair with a strange device on his head. Attached to it were a strange pair of goggles. His right hand was on a joy stick moving a telescope several feet away. He flipped up the visor, smiled, then flipped it back down. "I'm trying to focus the Z-1 Telescope on the comet but I can't seem to find it. It has to be within the Earth's atmosphere by now. I mean it's almost eleven fifteen. Where is it?"

Carry and Leanne simultaneously lifted their official TAC-oculars and scanned the sky. These were regular binoculars with a sticker on the side that read Team Adventure Club. Both noted that they only saw clouds and stars. Robbie was inputting numbers from one of the printers into a laptop Uncle Max had set up, making sure to record everything properly.

Carry lowered her TAC-oculars in time to see a limousine pull up. She wondered who it was. Then she noticed a black car pulling in behind the limo — two large men got out and walked to the limo, opening the door for a short, bald man in a suit followed by a very pretty woman. Several people started gawking at him, and one man even walked up to shake his hand and was promptly ushered away by one of the two men from the car.

Carry snapped a picture with her then pulled the memory card out and put it into her TAC COM. She enlarged the picture of the man and then double tapped to start a search. As soon as the Internet activated, it immediately recognized the image.

A news page popped up and Carry started reading about the man. It went on and on about Sir Oliver Hedgestone and his billions, and all the different types of companies he owned, from oil rigs to military weapons to service organizations. Carry continued to scroll, and more information popped up about his wife and the mysteries surrounding her disappearance.

"What did you find?" Leanne asked, causing Uncle Max and Robbie to look up.

"Oh, nothing. Just a rich billionaire with his limo on the beach." Carry flipped her TAC COM so Leanne could see it.

Uncle Max moved closer and looked at the image, then looked up the beach at the limo. "He's a tyrant!"

"Because he has money?" Carry asked.

"No, because he just fired like two hundred people from one of his companies last week." Uncle Max said. "Said he was putting more robots in his warehouses."

"Robots are cool!" Robbie said from behind the tarp.

"Be that as it may, it's not nice to replace hard working people with electronics. Trust me," Uncle Max said, lifting his binoculars. He too scanned the limo and the people around it. "Hedgestone has his fingers in the government too. Making personal shuttle carries for military personnel. They want to start the first Space Army. It's not going to work! Trust me! They have no idea what they're in for." Uncle Max said with a grunt.

Carry and Leanne looked at each other and smirked. Carry loved her uncle, and no matter what she wants to believe his story about being abducted and saving earth from an interstellar war, but sometimes she even doubted him herself. He did, however, know a lot about new devices and he built most of the stuff they use in the club and was teaching Robbie to build more. And he knew a lot about space travel. More than even her science teacher. But like her mom said; "You just don't know how much he's making up!" Could Uncle Max be making all this up and just a crazy goofball? Possibly. But either way Carry loved him. He was her goofball.

Uncle Max was busy studying Hedgestone when the monitors started to beep and buzz.

"There's something coming!" Robbie cried enthusiastically.

9

CHAPTER 9

The small comet burning through the atmosphere was white, and glowed brightly as it spiraled toward Belleview Heights. It was a hard rock with large craters all over it. The smoke billowing off the back was dark, as debris ripped from it and evaporated into moisture. The tip was super-heated, but instead of burning red it burned blue as it broke through the clouds.

Then something strange happened.

The comet's tip started spinning, and popped out a metal extension. A bright blue light shined from inside, and on each side a wing-shaped panel opened. The comet started to slow down as the wings tilted slightly.

Uncle Max watched the monitors zooming in his Z-1 telescope. He noticed the wings and his mouth fell open. He looked up and he could barely see it with his naked eye. Carry and Leanne, on the other hand, even zoomed in all the way on their TAC-oculars, could just see a blue ball hurling through the air with a large streaming dark tail.

Uncle Max darted to the back of his SUV and pulled out a large green trunk, dragging it back through the sand. He knelt down and stared at the digital combination lock, mind going blank. Carry and Leanne were too busy to notice he was even doing anything. Robbie, too, was in awe as he watched the comet up close on the monitor, but when he zoomed in, he saw a small flag on the comet that read; GREETING FROM THE PLANET ORT ORT. This gave him pause.

Most of the beach goers could barely make out the comet and were staring to point at the sky and murmur to each other. Sir Oliver Hedgestone was standing with his hands behind his back as he also watched. He was wearing dark sunglasses, but unlike the other watchers as he looked through them he could see the comet perfectly. Numbers scrolled on both lenses, calculating mass, velocity and other statistics. He could also see the message.

"Get Sergeant Collins on the phone. Now. We have an interesting specimen incoming, and an offer on the table."

Yes sir!" Jenny quickly pulled out her phone.

The military office was full of personnel looking at giant monitors and sitting behind desks with headsets on. There were fifty people, all either on the phone or talking on their headsets. The double doors to the room swung open, and a small man in military dress uniform walked in with a large red phone.

"Sergeant Collins, sir?"

A hulking sergeant turned around. He was six feet tall, with a flat top haircut, huge chin and long side burns that connected to his even fuller mustache. "You walk into my office in the middle of a training exercise, you better here to tell me we're under attack by aliens or giant robots!" he snarled.

The messenger held his eyes closed and handed him the phone. "It's... Sir Oliver Hedgestone. Sir."

Sergeant Collins snatched the phone. "DISMISSED!" He lifted the phone, watching the soldier scurry off. "What do you have for me?"

"Hold please." He recognized the voice as Hedgestone's current personal assistant.

He worked for the man with his branch of military personnel. He was often called on for more...delicate operation, and he was paid large sums of money to do it. In return, Hedgestone only called when it was important. This time was no different.

"We have something alien, Sergeant."

"How alien?" He raised an eyebrow at the thought.

"From another planet alien. I would hate to think it's an attack on the human race."

"Where?"

"Right in my back yard, serendipitously enough. I've already put my team on it. We will begin to try and collect it for observation." Sir Oliver Hedgestone's voice was smooth and controlled.

"We'll leave in ten."

"Excellent." The line went dead.

Collins looked around at the personnel in his office. "Jones, Tarrant, Khars, Bohn, Buchanan and Summers. We head out in five in full recon gear! Let's move people!" He bellowed across the room. "We've got an intergalactic threat on our hands!"

A few hundred yards down the beach, Uncle Max stared at the lock, trying to remember the combination. He tried to remember what he was doing when he was locking everything inside of this certain case. Was he in Africa? No. China? No. Bermuda? Yes! Bermuda, right after TAC fought that giant squid.

As Carry and Leanne watched, two silent helicopters appeared in the sky. They were huge and had Hedgestone Enterprises on the side in dark letters. The large side door opened, and two men in dark gear clipped their ropes to a guide and hung outside. The pilot maneuvered into position, obviously trying to line up their path with the comet. The second helicopter did the same thing.

As they got closer, one of the men hanging out a door held a long device with a clamp on one end, while another held a canister with a bio-hazard symbol on it.

"Do you see this?" Carry couldn't believe her eyes.

"Hedgestone Enterprises?" Leanne was glued to the scene as well.

"He's here for the comet. They're going to try and catch it!" Carry shouted.

Uncle Max spun in the sand and stood up. "What? No. They can't. No one can touch it!"

He looked at the closed case, then back across the beach to where Hedgestone was standing. He didn't have time to warn them. He had to make a choice — he knelt down again and punched in the code.

As the first helicopter approached the comet, the team let their lead lines go and dropped in the air. They steadied themselves over the comet, with the pilot matching their speed. They were only a few feet from the glowing alien rock. As they got a closer look one of them noticed the wings, but by that time it was too late.

"We might have an issue," He radioed to the others.

"What kind of issue?" The pilot responded.

"Not sure. Team two be ready."

"Team two ready," came the reply.

The soldier reached for the comet and managed to get the rope around it without touching it. He slowly closed the device around the comet and breathed easier. "Package secure."

Then the clamp started to freeze — and it didn't stop. The ice was working its way up the metal pole to his hand. Before he could do anything, his arm was frozen and in a blink, before he even had time to radio in, he was a solid block of ice.

"We have a problem!" His teammate screamed into the radio before he watched in horror as the ice came for him, too. The ice continued up the line to the helicopter itself; the blades stopped mid spin, and everything started to plummet to the ground.

Carry and Leanne watched as the helicopter glowed blue and then started to fall out of the sky. The comet burst through the device around it, and continued on its course. Team two pulled away, not even making an attempt to catch the comet themselves.

It was headed right for the bay. Carry and Leanne followed it with their TAC-oculars, watching in slack-jawed amazement as it hit the water, freezing it instantly. The comet bounced off the ice and back into the air before coming down again to hit a boat. That was also frozen solid, followed by the boardwalk. People started running, but everyone who got too close was frozen as well. As it continued to bounce and freeze, it began heading right for Sir Oliver Hedgestone.

He jumped back into the limo with Jenny right behind him, and they took off down the beach. They hit another car parked in the sand, but kept going, people jumping out of their way. The limo hit another vehicle and spun sideways, giving Jenny a good view out the window. She watched a nice young couple freeze solid. "It's freezing everything!"

"It seems it is."

The limo driver was doing his best trying not to hit things, but the ice was starting to catch up to them. He turned hard up a ramp, trying to get off the beach, but the wheels had already started to freeze.

Sir Oliver Hedgestone grabbed Jenny, and they jumped out, headed right for Carry and the rest of Team Adventure Club. Carry had stopped looking through her TAC-oculars and was now watching the billionaire run towards her. Then Jenny was frozen. Sir Oliver Hedgestone leapt into midair, but he, too, started to freeze. The case he was holding flipped opened and a huge red ruby flew through the air.

Carry watched as the bright red ruby spun through the air. The she realized the ice was coming right for her and the rest of Team Adventure Club. She grabbed her best friend, and they held each other, afraid they were going to freeze. But Uncle Max stood up suddenly and slammed a canister into the sand.

"Cover your eyes!" That was the only warning they got before the world exploded around them.

Carry blinked her eyes open to see a glowing force field around them. The ice moved up and around it, but left them safe. She then watched as the force field deflected the ice. It was only as the ruby bounced off with a 'TINK' that she realized the ruby itself was also unfrozen. It bounced off the sand and spun out onto the frozen ocean.

10

CHAPTER 10

The sunny seaside city of Belleview Heights was frozen solid in a matter of minutes. There wasn't a person, animal or building not encased in a frozen block of ice.

Most of the people were completely unaware of what had happened. Across town, Debra Valentine was sleeping comfortably in her bed, pink sleep mask pulled over her eyes, covers pulled tightly around her — even as she was encased in a cocoon of solid ice. They were all completely safe and soundly asleep for now, but if Carry and the gang didn't figure this case out and fast the entire world could be frozen forever.

The smoke settled inside their bubble, with Carry still holding tightly to Leanne. Robbie was standing with one foot up and his eyes covered. Uncle Max was breathing heavily. Carry and Leanne slowly let go of each other and stood up.

"What was that?" Carry asked.

"It's called an Omni-Directional Anti-Debris Deflector, otherwise known as the OD-ADD." Uncle Max looked around, pleased with himself.

"Not that. The thing bouncing around freezing our town?" Carry looked out at the frozen landscape

"That was bad news. I believe it is a missle from the planet Ort Ort. I think they may have just declared war on Earth."

Robbie, Carry and Leanne looked at him with mouths open. The only upside was that they finally knew, definitively, that all his stories about fighting aliens were true. Robbie found his voice first.

"What," he croaked.

"Robbie my boy, you have no idea what awaits us off this planet. Things so unimaginable and amazing you would need six lifetimes to look at it all." Uncle Max was starting to sort through his tools.

"So, when you said you fought to save Earth when you were a teenager? That was all true?" Carry tried to focus on her breathing.

"I wouldn't lie about such things. I was a hero once. Out there I'm a Captain of a starship! Here I'm a man-child people make fun of. It changes your outlook on the universe."

"I'm sorry." Carry said, tears starting to well up. How had she ever doubted him?

"Why? It's not your fault. Humans will never have any idea just how close they came to extinction. And it was me — a fifteen year old — who stopped it. Who fought the intergalactic battle for Earth. And all I was left with was my word. But, I know what I did, how I managed to lead a squadron of fighters against evil aliens and won. It's always been enough.."

Uncle Max lifted his shirt to show them a huge scar that ran from his shoulder to his elbow. "I got this when my fighters were the only ones left, and I had to go toe to toe with B'gan Kon Re Thras, the leader of the Salutatorians. A very evil race of Aliens from a 1000 light years away."

"Mom said you got that falling off the roof." Carry said.

"When I returned, we couldn't let anyone know what happened. So I swore to the Guthernians — a friendly race of aliens — that I would lie my scrawny little butt off. They fixed me up, and I came home. They had a huge celebration for me when I left. I was a grand hero. I hid the scar for a while, and when someone finally asked I said I did it years ago falling off the roof. No one said otherwise."

"So how do we stop this ice missle?" Carry stood up straighter. She was going to follow in Uncle Max's footsteps and be a great hero of Earth too.

"That is a good question." Uncle Max pulled out a long thin device from his weapons belt, turning the end of it. He pushed a red button and it hummed to life. He flipped the dark part of his goggles down and pointed the device at the shield. "Cover your eyes kids."

The device popped to life and started cutting through both the shield and the ice, etching out a nice doorway for them to walk through. The thick chunk of frozen ice slammed back into the frozen beach with a loud thud. As they stepped out into the world again the temperature changed drastically — it was getting cold quickly. Carry rubbed her arms as her breath escaped in a cloud of steam. Leanne and Robbie were also shivering, trying to hop around and rub their arms to get warm again.

"Over here guys." Uncle Max gestured for them to follow him to his van. With the laser, he etched the doors free and pulled out a large trunk. He started pulling out winter gear — all labeled with the TAC logo — and passing it around.

Once he was dressed in appropriate clothes, Robbie looked around. "Ah man! My skateboard is frozen!"

"Everything is frozen, Robbie! Look around!" Carry yelled.

"Not everything." He pointed to the ruby, sitting in the middle of the frozen ocean.

Carry turned to look, then then remembered seeing it fly out of the case Sir Oliver Hedgestone had been carrying. She carefully made her way out over the ice to retrieve it.

"Look how big it is Uncle Max!" She held it up with both hands.

Uncle Max put on his jacket as he made his way over to her. "Interesting." He accepted it from Carry and started to look closer. It was large for a ruby — or any other gem for that matter. The fact that it was still fine when everything else —everything he had fought to save so many years ago — was encased in ice meant something. He handed it to Robbie for safe keeping. "Put this in your bag and keep it close. Let's go see the damage."

Robbie pulled out a small tool and in flipped it back to reveal a hammer. He slammed it into the ice covering Leanne's scooter, but it just bounced off the ice and hit him square in the forehead. Robbie's feet went straight up into the air and he landed on his back. He gave a pathetic moan.

"Well, looks like we're walking." Uncle Max shrugged. "Robbie get up. This isn't the time to be taking naps."

Carry had moved to look at the frozen billionaire, and couldn't put her finger on why she felt like there was something strange about him. Perhaps she had seen him before? But where?

Uncle Max came over, putting an arm around her. "What's wrong?"

"I feel like I know him."

Sir Oliver Hedgestone stared back from inside his frozen prison. He couldn't make out their faces very well since the ice distorted his vision, but he made a note of everything he could. If only he could get out of the ice. He would get his ruby back.

"I've just got a bad feeling about this guy," Carry said as they all started the trek back toward town.

11

CHAPTER 11

Team Adventure Club looked in awe as they wandered around town. Everything and everyone was frozen solid. And it seemed to be getting colder by the minute. "Uncle Max we need to find some warm clothes. I'm freezing," Carry shivered, hugging her arms around herself.

"Let's head to the house and see if we can't get some clothes," Uncle Max said.

They cut through a yard and started on a trek through the back yards of the local neighborhoods. They hopped fence after fence, and even walked across someone's frozen pool. When they finally reached the house, they found it, too, covered in a layer of ice. Uncle Max pulled out a small laser gun and started cutting around the door. The entire door - along with a two inch thick ice block - fell back into the house with a thud.

Carry shook her head at her uncle before peering inside. She quickly went looking for her parents, finding her father looking in the bathroom mirror and brushing his teeth. Her mother was downstairs wearing bunny slippers and a bathrobe, a basket of laundry on her hip. Carry stared at her mother for a moment, poking her a few times and getting only a twinkling noise in return.

Then Carry noticed that her mother's eyes were moving. "Mom? Can you hear me?"

Her mother's eyes shot her a look. Carry shouted to Max, bringing him rushing over. "I think she can hear me!" They stared at each other and the mother-shaped ice block for a moment. "Should we cut her out?"

Max looked at his sister for along moment, before sighing. "Best not."

Carry swallowed, but nodded. "Yeah, she's safer in the ice." She turned to the ice block, putting one hand over where her mother's hand was frozen. "Mom, we will get you out of this. It's an alien attack. Don't worry. We will be right back!"

She ran upstairs and let out a grunt of frustration at finding all her clothes frozen too. She yelled again for Uncle Max, who made his way up the stairs, avoiding the slippery patches. He used his laser gun to shoot the closet a few times, freeing her clothes rack. A few of her shirts also incidentally caught on fire, making her yelp as she rushed to put it out. That done, she was finally able to liberate a her two biggest, fluffiest winter coats. She held them both up to show Leanne, who had come up to see what the commotion was all about. "Red or Blue?"

"Red!" Leanne grinned as Carry tossed her the coat.

Back outside and much warmer, they started to make their way up the street when four large black helicopters flew overhead. "Holy cow! Who are they?" Carry whispered as they ducked behind a frozen car.

"I was afraid of this. The military is already here. Which means we've got about an hour to find the alien weapon and destroy it before they get their hands on it." Uncle Max watched the helicopters disappear over the hill before starting them all moving again..

"Why do we need to destroy it?" Leanne asked.

"If the military gets their hands on it they will try to use it against our enemies."

"So...." Robbie looked at him, genuinely confused.

"If the weapon gets into our enemies hands instead, the whole planet is doomed. It's better if no one has it," Uncle Max pointed out. "Everyone off the street. We have to move under cover now."

They made it to Robbie's house unnoticed, and Max stopped just outside the door, looking off in the direction the helicopters had disappeared to. It was a good guess that the military was setting up a temporary base not too far away; several helicopters hovered were hovering over one area, and they could see men rappelling down out of them. Max pulled out a small plastic contact lens case.

He put the lenses in, blinking a few times to settle them and activate the technology. They magnified his vision, allowing him to zoom in and out by blinking. Max watched the military men pulling out equipment as they began setting up their camp. This was going to be a race to try and get to the weapon before anyone else.

"Max, laser!" Robbie called from inside the house, shaking him out of his musings

Blinking a few times to return the lens to regular vision, he headed inside to help the final member of the team get his own winter gear unfrozen. He found him looking longingly around the room. "It's all ruined. All my comics. All my posters. All ruined."

Max patted him on the shoulder, both of them giving a moment of silence for the lost precious reading materials.

Finally, Robbie sighed. "C'mon! Let's go do whatever it is where going to stop this stupid freeze rocket piece of junk." As he walked, it was obvious he had forgotten that the floor was icy as well; he slipped and was suddenly down the hallway, down the staircase and straight out the front he had left opened.

Carry and Leanne both watched, eyes wide, as Robbie went sliding past them. Both of them looked up at Max, who was more carefully coming down the stairs. "We need to stop him. He could slide for days!"

"Days?!" Carry's eyes widened.

"Well, maybe not days. But he very well could slide to the next county."

Meanwhile, Robbie was trying to maintain his composure as he accelerated down the street and through town. He tried using his feet as a brake, but it was no use. He then tried to grab something as he zipped along, but that proved to be unhelpful as well; everything was still covered in ice and just slipped right out of his hands. He then decided to focus on where exactly he was going. It took a few heartbeats before he registered what he was seeing. The ice had made a launch ramp of sorts off the water tower, and he was headed right for it.

Robbie watched helplessly as he slid into impending doom. He hit the ice ramp and was shot out over the top of the water tower, screaming and flailing his arms and legs like a dancing chicken. He tried turning his body so he could see where he might land, but just as he got himself turned around he started the fall portion of this little trip. Right back toward the slide. He came down fast, hitting the slide and getting launched back the way he came.

Down the street, Max, Leanne and Carry watched his progress. "We've got to do something," Max said, watching Robbie start his return voyage at twice the speed he had when he left.

They all looked around, seeing no immediate solutions. As Robbie came barreling by, they had no choice but to jump out of the way. They could only watch helplessly as he hit the side of a house and was launched upside down to another house, which launched him back down the street.

He was being bounced around, so this time, they positioned themselves right in his path. Max dropped to his knees and assumed a catchers stance, but Carry pulled him right back up again. "Uncle Max, that won't work; it will just cause one of you to get hurt! We need redirection. If his trajectory and speed can be matched by opposite trajectory and reduced speed we can slow him down. Decrease his inertia exponentially."

Leanne's mouth fell open.

"Math class?" Carry shrugged. She looked down the street all of sudden she could see "math vision" again. The distance of Robbie from her to everything around, the curvature of the street lights and trees, and even the angle she needed to create triangles from their positions. "Uncle Max, shoot the ice off that tree branch!"

Once he did, she started gesturing quickly. "Do you have any rope or elastic?"

He dug around his pockets, pulling out a ball of rubber bands. "What about this!"

"That won't work. We need a thick rope to snag Robbie."

"This has the tensile strength of a dying sun. It can stop a freight train at full speed." He tossed it to Carry.

"It's exceptionally light," she gave him a skeptical look.

"Space Wire," Max smirked.

Carry shrugged and went to work, quickly making a snare of sorts for Robbie to get caught in. "Okay, we need to make a ramp with the curvature of thirty-two degrees and negative invert of sixteen degrees to a forty-five degree angel at the top for him to shoot into the air."

"On it!" Max shouted. He started shooting the ice, creating a slushy in the street. He and Leanne pushed it together like playdoh until they had a solid ramp.

As Robbie came speeding onto the street, he hit the Space Wire. It snagged him, and like some kind of cartoon roadrunner trap his momentum took him swinging up over the ramp and around the tree, over and over until there was no more slack and he was finally still, bound to the tree..

Robbie was motionless for a moment, blinking at all of them. "THAT WAS THE MOST AMAZING ROLLER COASTER IN THE WORLD! WAAAA WHOOOOO!" He did as much of a happy dance as he could against the tree, laughing. "You should have seen how I high I went into the air! It was amazing! I could see the next town!"

Max shot the wire, freeing Robbie who slid to the ground, shaking his head. "Guys! You should try that! Holy moly! It was...the best thing ever!"

Carry and Leanne gave him looks while Uncle Max helped him to his feet. "Oh, and I saw Mrs. Keller's dog Pogo! Don't let me forget that," he said as they walked away.

12

CHAPTER 12

A large Hedgestone B-45 Pelican Helicopter landed on the ice several yards away from the impromptu military base. The rear door opened and ten soldiers got out, followed by Sergeant Collins. He popped a cigar in his mouth, lighting it up as he strolled down the ramp.

In a field not far away three military jeeps, six military TR-99 Supercobra attack helicopters, two EW-134 Apache Fire Strikes speed choppers and various other modes of transportation were lined up, waiting for his arrival.

First Lieutenant Tarrant came to attention and saluted smartly. "Sergeant, welcome to Rosewood base."

"You boys go set up your stations, and I'll see you in a few. Do me proud men!" Sergeant Collins bellowed.

"You heard him men! Khars and Buchanan - move the gear to the armory. Jones, Bohn and Summers - follow me." Tarrant barked out orders, getting everyone moving swiftly to their assigned tasks.

As the grunts scattered, another soldier came closer. "Sergeant Collins! Captain Antonio Hernandiez. Glad to meet you. If you'll follow me, Sir, I will escort you to the command tent."

As they walked, Sergeant Collins took a deep breath. "I miss the smell of wet canvas and weapons."

"Yes, Sir. It is a distinct smell."

They arrived at the largest tent in the complex, located in the center of the camp, a soldier on either side of the door standing guard.

The Captain gave another salute before heading back to his own duties. As he entered, Sergeant Collins was met by two older men in military uniforms. He saluted them, nodding as they returned the greeting. "Colonel Richardson, Colonel Frierson."

Pleasantries over, Colonel Richardson tossed a packet of papers onto the table that had Top Secret stamped on the cover. "This is a mess on a global level Collins. We have to keep this under wraps. No one must know about this."

Sergeant Collins opened up the packet, skimming the contents. He paused when he came to a sheet of codes for a nuclear strike, with the words OPERATION CLEAN HOUSE at the top.

He raised an eyebrow and tilted the sheet so the Colonels could see. "Operation Clean House?"

"You have twelve hours to sort this mess out, find the alien artifact and get your soldiers out of here. Then Mr. Clean comes in." Colonel Frierson said.

"And the residents of the town?"

"In war - be it domestic, international or galactic - we risk collateral damage. The needs of the many outweigh the needs of the few. A certain amount of civilian casualties are expected. We have run the numbers, and the predicated losses are acceptable." Colonel Frierson lit up a pipe, taking a long drag.

Sergeant Collins took a drag of his own cigar before nodding. "Consider it done." He continued flipping through the paperwork, pulling out one that read Complete Deniability.

Colonel Frierson noted what he was looking at, and nodded. "That's insurance. Once we nuke the town, we'll say it was a gas main leak. We will, of course, be very sorry for everyone's loss."

"The press secretary is already working on a speech for the president for tomorrow," Colonel Richardson added.

"War! It's a damn shame it doesn't happen all the time!" Sergeant Collins bounced on his toes.

"Sergeant, with that attitude you'll be a Colonel before you know it," Colonel Frierson clapped him on the back, and he followed his fellow Colonel out of the tent, leaving Sergeant Collins to his work.

He left the tent as well, and he made his way across the camp to the communication tents. First Lieutenant Tarrant was inside the main pavillion waiting for him. "Sergeant, communications are a go, and connection with the Hedgestone Satellite has been established. However, we have not secured communication with Sir Oliver Hedgestone himself."

"If you can't establish communication with him, then get your men out there and find him."

"We have already triangulated his location, Sir." One of the men manning the tent pointed to a screen. "He seems to be sitting on the beach. He hasn't moved in twenty minutes."

"If you know where he is then send someone to go get him," Sergeant Collins snapped.

13

CHAPTER 13

Team Adventure Club made their way across town, bypassing major roads and cutting through back alleys and side streets as they worked their way to the military camp. They were amazed that one small alien projectile could do so much damage. Every structure, person, vehicle and thing was covered in a thick sarcophagus of ice.

Robbie's wrist communicator suddenly beeped. Radar showed an oncoming vehicle headed their way. "Everybody down!" They all dove into bushes on the side of the road, waiting until long after the Jeep cruised by to re-emerge.

"That was close!" Leanne stared back toward the beach where the Jeep had disappeared.

Once they were within a few blocks of the camp, they started to hear the commotion of the busy soldiers now. The ambient light coming off the base camp gave an eerie glow to that side of town. Max looked at his TAC COM checking for movement nearby. "Coast is clear."

They kept moving, sticking to the shadows to avoid being noticed. They finally made it to a huge house just across the street from the base camp, where they took a moment to regroup. "Uncle Max. What's the plan once we get in?" Carry asked.

"We find the alien device."

"Then what? We can't touch it, remember?" Leanne rubbed at her arms – the temperature was continuing to drop as time went on.

"I haven't figured that part out yet," Uncle Max sighed.

"Well, if we can't touch it then that means the military can't touch it either," Robbie pointed out.

"True." Uncle Max patted him on the back. "I could get next to it and toss an OD-ADD down, and then it would be contained inside that."

"With you. And then what?" Carry asked. "You would be stuck inside your magic shield bubble forever!"

Uncle Max started to respond, then froze. "Shhh." He motioned to everyone to freeze. His TAC COM didn't show anything, but he didn't want to risk it.

"Do you hear footsteps?" Leanne whispered.

But then it was too late. Uncle Max turned and a team of men suddenly appeared before them. Carry and Leanne both screamed and Robbie smacked his communicator. "I thought you said these things detected life forms Max!"

"Freeze!" one of the soldiers yelled.

They all stopped moving, until Robbie began giggling.

"Something funny boy?" The soldier glared at him.

"You said freeze. Everything is frozen. Classic!" Robbie continued to chuckle.

Carry nudged him giving him a glare.

"Everyone shut up and stop moving!" the soldier yelled again. He motioned to one of his comrades, "call this in. We need a transport."

"Listen, can't you let the kids go and just take me in," Uncle max peered at the name patch sewn onto the soldier's uniform, "Mr. Pegg?"

"It's Officer Pegg, and I'm afraid not. We have to take you all in. I'll make sure you're treated right." Officer Pegg looked at Carry and Leanne; his face and voice softened a bit. "Ladies it's ok. We're not going to hurt you. We're just on a routine surveillance mission. As you can see something very strange is going on."

They all stood around and waited for a few minutes until another Jeep arrived. "I'm going to need all of you to get in please," Officer Pegg gestured to the car.

"It's okay guys. Let's do this and they'll let us go in a while." Uncle Max said.

Robbie raised his eyebrows, but he didn't comment. This wasn't the first time Team Adventure Club had been taken into custody by a military unit. Several months ago they were on a quest in Mexico researching the Mayan pyramids and found what Carry still believes to be the entrance to El Dorado. But they had been stopped by the Mexican government and asked to leave the country without incident.

Carry suddenly realized where she knew the frozen man from. He was the same guy who had been with the Mexican officials. It had to be! She remembered his bald head and his nose. She kept quiet about her revelation as they all boarded the transport vehicle.

The Jeep headed into the camp, and Max paid close attention to how it was all laid out. He noted that they had found where the sphere had finally stopped, with spotlights set up all around it. There were close to twenty soldiers frozen in place - each one bent over as if they had tried to pick it up. Then the Jeep turned a corner and he lost sight of the artifact and went back to cataloging each tent, truck and landmark along the way.

They finally arrived at a small tent near the center of camp, where they were directed to disembark. "Stand in line and don't move," Officer Pegg said. He was reporting something on his radio, but it was too soft for any of TAC to make out.

Finally, Officer Pegg nodded and signed off. "Officer Green, please take the young man into tent six."

"Wait. What?" Robbie's eyes went wide.

"Don't worry just protocol."

"Really? To take a twelve year old boy into a military tent alone?" Uncle Max moved closer, trying to look protective.

"We have to locate his guardian. Unless that's you?"

"Well, technically no." Uncle Max said.

"Are you any of these children's guardian?" Officer Green had pulled out a notebook.

"He's my uncle," Carry chimed in. "These are my friends."

Officer Pegg nodded, gesturing for Officer Green to move forward. "It'll be fine, son. Just go with this officer."

Before Robbie could get sarcastic, two female officers came closer, and

Officer Pegg gestured to Carry and Leanne. "Officer Cardone and Officer Humphrey, take these two young ladies into tent four."

"No. I want to stay with my Uncle Max," Carry grabbed Max's arm.

"I'm sorry, but for now that isn't possible," Officer Pegg gave her another kind look.

"These children were put under my temporary care by their parents. I won't allow them to be taken from me. It would be very irresponsible of me," Uncle Max held out his arms, and all of TAC moved close.

"I understand, but I'm just doing my job," Officer Pegg noted. "And right now, I have orders to send you to three different tents."

"Officer Pegg, I respect the military and the police, but if any of these children leave my sight for one second I will call down a wrath of universal devastation!" Uncle Max held his chin up high.

"What are you saying exactly?" Officer Pegg's eyes narrowed, and he suddenly looked less friendly.

"Exactly as it sounded."

"I can put you in jail for the rest of your life. You know that right?"

"You try and do anything to these kids and jail won't be enough for me. I know some very influential people!" Uncle Max pulled himself to his full height, trying to look intimidating.

"Take him to tent ten." Officer Pegg rolled his eyes and gestured to another officer who had been standing by.

"I'm warning you." Uncle Max knew it was hopeless, but at least it was distraction enough that none of them were searched as the soldiers grabbed them and started dragging them all to separate tents. It was something. For now.

14

CHAPTER 14

The tent was bright and smelled like old shoes. Robbie sat behind a huge foldaway table, a single plastic glass of water in front of him. He was busy looking around cataloging everything he could when a man in a military uniform, wearing huge brown glasses with thinning hair combed over on top strolled in.

The officer sat down in front of Robbie, placing a yellow folder on the table between them. He stared for a moment, and Robbie stared right back. Finally, he flipped open the folder and cleared his throat. "Robert Whitman?"

"Yes sir."

"I'm Sergeant Victor Dillion. I'm a psychiatrist, sociologist and deviant profiler."

Robbie just started again.

"Are your parents are Robert Andrew Whitman and Jenna Elizabeth Teliaford-Whitman?"

"Yes sir."

"You have a sister? Rebecca Jenna Whitman. "Disabled?"

"Yes sir."

"Your address is 13244 E. Spring Creek Ln Belleview Heights 453661?"

"Yes sir."

"So tell me Robert, why were you with your friends tonight?"

"We went to the beach to watch the meteor shower."

"So you were at the beach at one in the morning?"

"Yes sir."

"Why?"

Robbie gave them man an incredulous look. "I just told you. To watch the meteor shower."

"So you did. Who is Maximilian Bonnefield to you?"

"Uncle Max? He's my like my uncle." Robbie knew some attitude was starting to creep into his tone. No sense jumping the guy before he got as much information from this guy as he could though.

"He is like your uncle or he is your uncle?" Sergeant Dillion was making notes as they spoke.

"Well, we're not related if that's what you mean. He's Carry's real uncle and my adopted uncle."

"How's the water?"

Robbie blinked at the sudden change in topics. "Wet."

"You want a soda?"

"Can I?" Robbie Sat forward, bouncing in his seat a bit. He loved soda.

"Of course."

Robbie leaned back again; there was something wrong with that smile. Robbie found himself starting to become a little afraid. The guy was more than creepy - he was right out of a late night horror movie. Sergeant Dillion stood up suddenly and exited the room, but Robbie barely had time to sigh with relief before he returned with a glass of soda, ice bobbing around inside. He placed it in front of Robbie, who was distracted by a ring he was wearing. It was gold and black, with a sword and shield symbol on one side and an emerald on top. The man sat back down, creepy smile plastered on again Robbie just awkwardly looked away.

"Drink your soda Robbie. It's okay. It's not poisoned." Sergeant Dillion watched him intently.

Robbie made eye contact again, giving him an incredulous look. His mind began to whirl. Who says things like that? People who poison things, that's who. Robbie stared at the glass, not reaching for it.

The officer pushed the glass of soda closer to Robbie. "Drink."

Robbie decided to say to hell with it. He was going to show this guy that he wasn't afraid to take a sip of soda while possibly under arrest by the military and facing three years of being grounded when he parents found out. This just may be his last soda ever. He took a sip, surprised it was good. So he drank a little more. If there was poison, he couldn't taste it. He shrugged and thinking here goes nothing, downed the whole glass. "Where are my friends?"

"Oh, you mean the little girls and that odd fellow, Maximilian?" Sergeant Dillion gave another toothy smile.

"No, the elephant and the dragon!" Robbie was starting to lose his patience.

"Well, well, get some sugar in you, and you get feisty."

"Listen, it's been a long night, I'm tired, the town is frozen solid, and I spent about ten minutes on the craziest ride of my life. I'd like to get home, take a shower and go to bed, so I can go to school tomorrow." Robbie tried to look stern.

"Well, this is a dilemma. The entire town is frozen solid, except four people. You, the girls and the spaceman."

"Spaceman? You mean Uncle Max?" Robbie blinked.

"Once you've been to space, you can be called a spaceman. I assume."

"Uncle Max has been to space?"

"Oh, very much so. In fact we owe him a great bit of gratitude for saving us from the aliens so many years ago."

"Are you joking?" Robbie eyed the man carefully, looking for signs of crazy. Well, more signs anyway.

Sergeant Dillion went back to staring for a moment, not saying anything. Robbie was starting to get very uncomfortable again. Finally, Sergeant Dillion took a deep breath, jotting down a few notes before looking back up at Robbie. "Another soda perhaps?"

"Yes, please. And cookies." Robbie brightened.

"I'll see what I can do."

Sergeant Dillion exited again, and this time, as soon as he was gone, Robbie sprang from his chair and immediately started looking for a way out. He tried pulling the bottom of the tent up, but it was heavy and made of canvas. Robbie pulled his trusty one-of-a-kind TAC survival knife out of his boot and was about to cut his way to freedom when Sergeant Dillion returned. Robbie turned quickly secreted his knife away and pretended to have just been stretching his legs. It was going to be a long night.

15

CHAPTER 15

Max was sitting in front of four high ranking military officials, all heroes of one sort or another. The oldest, sitting at the table, was, like Max himself, a space hero. He had also participated in the galactic battle for Earth so many years ago, and was also sworn to secrecy.

They have enough problems as it was. The last thing they needed was for the entire planet to know about space aliens and intergalactic wars. But Max, and the officer now charged with questioning him, Colonel Henry Alexander Roberts, knew the truth, along with a select group of military and government officials. Like the President of the United States.

"Maximilian Bonnefield, we meet again." Colonel Roberts was giving him a piercing stare.

Max nodded. "It seems so."

"You want to explain what is happening?"

"Alien artifact crash landed, turning this town to ice. Can't pick it up. Can't touch it. Turns everything to ice." Max summed up the situation.

"We learned that the hard way." Colonel Roberts rubbed a hand across his face. He looked tired. "How can we stop this?"

"I was in the middle of working that out when your MPs decided to bring us in." Max said.

"We've tried everything just short of a nuclear explosion." Another of the men standing listening contributed.

Max shook his head. "Honestly, I don't know. I've never encountered a device like this before. I need to get a closer look to come up with any answers."

"We are flying in a team of scientists from Washington to take a look at it." Another of the officers looked smug at that declaration.

"You can fly in a hundred scientists, they're not going to figure it out any time soon." Max narrowed his eyes. "And in the meantime we have an entire town of people who need to become unfrozen immediately."

"Well, as in all cases such as this, the people are the least of our worries. We must learn more about the artifact and discover its possibilities." The smug officer leaned back, looking for all the world like he had just made some kind of profound announcement.

Max was not impressed. "Like how you can manipulate it to use as weapon?"

The room fell silent for a moment. Colonel Roberts at least looked a bit apologetic. He knew the stakes, but he had to play the game if he wanted to keep his position. And right now, that meant toeing the party line, so to speak. "We understand we owe you a lot a gratitude, but this situation is out of your hands. We will have to wait until our team of scientists arrive before we can proceed. And that means keeping you and the children in custody. Unfortunately."

"If you let the people of the town sit on ice much longer it might cost them their lives. Let the children go and I'll work with you to uncover how the artifact works myself," Max pleaded softly. He knew if he could get TAC out there, they could come up with something.

"You said yourself, we can bring in a hundred scientists and it won't matter. Why would you be any different?" The smug officer was sneering at him again. Max decided he really didn't like that guy. At all.

He knew Colonel Smug was likely with the Alien Intelligence Agency, and he badly wished he had the wrist communicator they had taken away from him. In fact they took all his devices – unlike the kids, they knew he was a threat. He needed a plan, so he gave them a big smile. "I might have an idea."

"Continue." Colonel Roberts tapped a pen on the table.

"We picked up a ruby that was also unaffected by the ice. It might be worth looking at." Max said.

"A ruby? Why would that work?" Officer Smug just kept barging into the conversation. Colonel Roberts was starting to look as annoyed as Max felt.

"When the artifact landed and started freezing everything, the ruby was the only thing left unfrozen. I found it on the ground, unharmed." Max spoke slowly, enunciating each word carefully.

"It didn't freeze?" Colonel Roberts jumped back in.

"It didn't even get cold. It was like the ice avoided it." Max let his voice return to normal.

"Where is it now?" Colonel Roberts made a few quick notes.

"Your men probably locked it up with the rest of my stuff. Which, by the way, I will want back."

"You'll get your stuff back once we see if this ruby really exists or not." Colonel Smug leaned forward against the table, pointing a finger at Max.

"Why would I lie about a ruby?" Max was beyond frustrated with this idiot.

"Why not?" Colonel Smug rolled his eyes and gave another superior expression.

Max leaned forward himself, getting annoyed beyond his ability to hide it. "Well, for one I have nothing to hide. I didn't freeze the town!"

"Who knows what you're capable of Mr. Bonnefield," The irritating Colonel sneered at him.

Max gave the Colonel a toothy smile. He glanced at another of the officers who had been silent the entire time. That one, he knew, was a war hero and veteran, and had fought bravely in Vietnam, Cuba and Saudi Arabia. It was that one he addressed his answer to. "The sad truth, Secret Inspector Bonnefield, is that you don't. Isn't that right, Dad?"

"Don't I know it, son." Secret Inspector Bonnefield sighed, breaking his silence for the first time. They shared a secret smile. "Now, where is my granddaughter?"

16

CHAPTER 16

Carry and Leanne sat holding hands as they waited in a large white tent. A female officer stood silently in the corner keeping watch, totally unaware that Carry and Leanne were talking in code via taps on their palms. They could hold complete conversations about anything and everything using this method, and often did in class. Once, on a mission, Leanne was able to find Carry in a cave by using their code. Robbie, however, wasn't allowed to use the code anymore. He couldn't spell, and half the time his messages for help came out as declaring various animals were stuck in cheese. The best one was when he said the clown had lost his cheese and there was a dragonfly eating all the mustard butts.

Right now they were strategizing on how to get out of the tent and find Robbie and Uncle Max. In the middle of their planning, the tent door swished opened and an older Colonel walked in. Carry jumped up and smiled. "Grandpa?!"

Her grandfather nodded to the officer who had been guarding them. "You are dismissed."

The woman saluted and exited the tent as Max stepped in. Carry and Leanne's faces lit up as they ran for him. Max kneeled hugging the girls. "I'm fine. How did they treat you?" Max asked.

"Fine. No one came in or out. We just sat here for like an hour with the quiet lady in the corner." Carry said. "Where's Robbie?"

"He's with an Alien Intelligence Agent in tent 27." One of the agents who had come in with Max and Grandpa chimed in.

"Why on earth is he with AIA personnel?" Max asked.

"Good question. I didn't order that." Secret Inspector Bonnefield's eyes narrowed.

"Under protocol 687 of the intergalactic earth code and paragraph 79 article 4 section 6.3, any person or persons detained in the event of an alien-terrorist invasion or domestic threat shall be remanded into custody until AIA Agents feel said person is human with no intentions of earth threat." Colonel Smug cited.

Secret Inspector Bonnefield gave him a hard look, until the snug seemed to melt away. "I'll just go acquire him for you, Colonel."

"Good Idea." Secret Inspector Bonnefield snapped. "Bring him to the mess hall, I'm sure everyone is hungry."

They walked through a winding series of tents until Carry stopped in her tracks, making Leanne slam into her. "What's wrong?" Leanne asked.

"Look!" Carry said in a whisper. She pointed between the tents to where two men were unloading the still-frozen form of the man from the beach. The one Carry was now more certain than ever had been in Mexico as well. The girls shared a look, both of them knowing this was probably not good news.

They quickly caught up to the rest of the group, going inside the mess tent, which was one of the largest in camp. There were a least fifty tables set up with soldiers all eating, laughing, talking, playing cards and relaxing. Everything came to a screeching halt as Secret Inspector Bonnefield walked in. Almost in sync, everyone stood up and saluted him, standing at attention until he waved them down.

They got to go to the front of the line and were given all the food they wanted, piled high. They were all starving, so they sat down with overflowing plates, ready to dig in. As they found a table and got settled, Robbie was escorted into the room by a strange man. Robbie ran to the table, and Carry and Leanne got up and hugged him hard. He looked around tom. "What is going on?"

"Robbie meet my grandfather, Secretary of Defense and Secret Inspector Theodore Bonnefield and Colonel Henry Alexander Roberts." Carry said.

Robbie blinked, then saluted, getting smiles and salutes from both men. He knew the name Henry Alexander Roberts - Max had spoken very highly of him on more than one occasion. And he had read his book the "Article 42: The real answer" about the military and the possibilities of alien life forms, and what the government was trying to do to make sure everyone got along. "Colonel Roberts, your book was amazing," he managed to stutter out, awestruck.

"Thank you young man." Colonel Roberts smiled again.

Robbie spent another moment basking that one of his heroes knew who he was before he looked down at all the food. And frowned. "Where's my dinner?"

"Please help yourself Robbie." Secret Inspector Bonnefield pointed to the buffet. Robbie wasted no time complying. He was starving, and had his eye on some meatloaf.

17

CHAPTER 17

The room was buzzing with hair dryers. Ten soldiers wielding two hair dryers each attempted to thaw Sir Oliver Hedgestone and his assistant from the ice. It was a slow going, but it seemed to be working. The room however was nearing 110 degrees; Sergeant Collins walked in and walked right back out again. "Holy Hot Pocket! It's like a Greek sauna in there."

He motioned to the Captain who was in charge of Operation Thaw. "Come and get me once they are de-iced. I'll be in my tent."

Before he could take more than a few steps, however, a young private came running up. "Sir, there is an issue."

"What kind of issue?" Sergeant Collins narrowed his eyes.

"Well...sir...it seems the four suspects have been released."

"What?" The private fidgeted a bit as Sergeant Collins' voice went flat.

"Well...sir, Secret Inspector Bonnefield and the AIA are in the mess tent eating with them now."

Sergeant Collins started to turn purple.

"And, ah, that's not all sir. Apparently, they are related to him in some capacity."

"And what capacity would that be?"

Swallowing hard, the private took a few tries to get his voice working again. "One of the children seems to be his grandchild and the strange crazy guy is well...his son. Sir."

Sergeant Collins just stared at him for a long moment, making the private sweat. "Very well. Thank you private, you are dismissed.".

He made his way back to his own tent. He needed to figure out what this meant to their operations. As he flipped the light on, he suddenly realized he wasn't alone. Two AIA agents were sitting in his chairs. "Ah, Sergeant Collins. We have many things to discuss. I am agent Coopee and this is my partner Agent Lasko ."

Sergeant Collins looked them over. Coopee was thin and balding and was overly pale. Lasko was shorter, thicker and blonde. "Do we now?"

Sergeant Collins pulled out a fat cigar out of his pocket, lighting it up and motioning for the agents to start talking.

"We have heard that you are a man who can get things done. There is a man named Maximilian Bonnefield currently in your camp. He causes problems with our agency and its credibility.." Agent Coopee said evenly, not appearing to be bothered by the smoke being blown his way..

"Can I assume he is also the son of Secret Inspector Bonnefield, the Secretary of Defense for the United States?" Sergeant Collins smirked at them, pleased he could show off that he was informed as well.

Agent Coopee nodded, a small smile forming.

"And what is it you would like me to help with, exactly?"

"We would like you to... take care of the problem."

"Assassinate him?" Sergeant Collins asked flatly.

"That's such an ugly word. We would like to remove the threat. We are willing to make some... necessary adjustments for you as compensation for your help."

"Necessary adjustments?"

"You are a very capable officer – you should have command of your own base. Which would, of course, come with a ver dignified increase in pay. Perhaps a comprehensive retirement package to look forward to once you find you are ready to leave this life behind. For example." Agent Coopee gave him another nearly non-existent smile.

Sergeant Collins snorted. "I've been in the military far too long to know when I'm getting the fat end of a short stick."

The agents looked at each other for a long moment, before Coopee handed him a folder. Inside was picture of his oldest son, Freddy, along with a recommendation letter to Harvard University from the President of the United States. "What is this?"

"Just another example of how we can help you, Sergeant. Your entire family could have a very comfortable, profitable life. All in exchange for one simple task."

He stared at the folder for a long moment before a wicked smile grew. "Where do I sign?"

"No signatures required, Sergeant. The moment Maximilian Bonnefield ceases to be a problem, you will find you – and your family – moving up in life."

"How do I know you won't back out of the deal?" Sergeant Collins tossed the folder on his table and gave the agents another hard look.

"You have our word. Your son will go to Harvard on a football scholarship. From there he will find himself recruited to his NFL team of choice. You will find your promotion and reassignment paperwork immediately being processed. I think you will find yourself on, as they say, easy street." Agent Coopee stood up, holding out a hand, and the two shook firmly.

"Gentleman, Mr. Bonnefield will be... retired... before the ink dries on the scholarship paperwork."

"We are counting on you, Sergeant Collins. Do not let the AIA down."

18

CHAPTER 18

The helipad was chaotic with activity as Max, Carry, Leanne and Robbie watched Secret Inspector Bonnefield and his team – including Colonel Roberts - depart. Max waved and gave everyone a hearty smile and thumbs up, but he was concerned. There were a lot of men still in camp who he knew would actively work against them, and with the Secretary of Defense no longer in residence, it opened up the door to trouble.

Speaking of which, Max turned to see several agents he knew wanted him out of the picture. Permanently if they could find a way to manage it. He immediately put himself between the children and the agents. "Agent Coopee, Agent Lasko, Agent Dillion. I didn't realize you were on location."

"We are here for the rather unusual ruby you seem to have... acquired, Mr. Bonnefield," Agent Coopee had always struck him as slimy. He strongly suspected the man was not what he pretended to be, but thus far he hadn't managed to uncover any evidence.

For now, though, he would play along. It wasn't just his own well-being he needed to worry about, but the children and an entire town of frozen people. "Take me to my stuff and you'll get it."

"Of course. Right this way."

The agents led them to another tent full of boxes and crates. On the ground someone had written "Property of the US Government; Carry Calusa" on several of the boxes. Carry yelped, "My stuff! The government doesn't own my things!" She ran over and started to open one of the boxes. Agent Lasko grabbed her arm, pulling so hard it made her cry out.

Max smacked the agent's hand off of Carry, spinning the man's arm behind his back before he could react. "Don't ever touch her again, or I'll rip this chicken bone you call an arm off and use it as a crochet mallet." Max didn't rarely drop his affable, goofy oddball persona, but no one was going to hurt his charges. No one.

Agent Coopee placed his hand on Max's shoulder. "Please let go of the official military personnel you are currently assaulting."

"Assaulting! That bozo nearly broke my arm!" Carry sniffed.

"You know, little children can be locked up, too. And lost forever. Do you want to be placed in a home for young boys?" Agent Coopee sneered at Robbie, who had moved to help Max. .

"No." Robbie said, looking away. For the first time in a long while he was frightened. He didn't know what these men where up to. He didn't trust any of them, and they had the means to make them all disappear. He wished this case was chasing ancient warriors through the jungle. Or even better - Bigfoot or the Loch Ness Monster. Robbie had faced all of those with less fear than he had now. Well maybe not Loch Ness. That was a huge monster, and he's pretty sure none of Team Adventure Club will ever be allowed back into Scotland. Ever.

Max let the agent go and stepped back, looking down at Robbie. He was furious the agent had scared him, and he knew the man was doing it on purpose. Max gave the agent a hard look, but he didn't say anything. He found his box and took his stuff back, then deliberately took all of the boxes with the children's names on them, pulled out the items and handed them out, daring any of the agents to stop him. None of them moved.

As a team, all three put their TAC COMs and brought them back online. "Welcome Team. Synchronization is complete. Heartbeats are slightly elevated but within normal parameters. Proceed normally."

The agents looked impressed, despite themselves. "What is that you have there?"

"Intellectual property, Agent Coopee. Back off." Max gave him a toothy smile.

"That looks like alien technology to me, Mr. Bonnefield." Agent Dillion moved closer.

"It also shoots lasers if you really want to find out." Max pointed his device at them..

"We are all on the same side." Agent Dillion hadn't taken his eyes off the TAC COMs.

"Are we?" Leanne asked. She was usually the quiet one, but if she needed to say something she did. The agents looked at her, arms folded as she waited for an answer. There was none. "That's what I thought."

"The ruby? Where is it?" Agent Coopee changed the subject.

Max gave a sly smile and reached over, pulling it out of the agent's own pocket. When he had been in the interrogation room, he held the ruby in his hand, cloaked until he was addressed by Agent Coopee - who made it more than easy to slip it into his pocket. The agent was so distracted with his own ego he hadn't felt it happen.

With a hard look, Agent Coopee reached for it. Max snatched it back, keeping it just out of reach. "Give me the ruby, Mr. Bonnefield. Now."

"I can carry it to where ever you want to use it." Max smirked.

"We will be taking it to our lab." Agent Coopee said. "I am afraid you are not allowed on those premises."

Agent Lasko gave a meaningful look at the children, who were standing in awe that Max had managed to keep the ruby safe by hiding it on one of the "bad guys" without him knowing. Max wasn't willing to risk them. Just as he was about to hand it over, Sergeant Collins burst in with Sir Oliver Hedgestone.

"There they are! Team Adventure Club! They stole my ruby!"

Carry looked at Leanne with a huff. "Oh great! Here we go again."

"I think we should run." Robbie said.

19

CHAPTER 19

They fell out of the tent in a jumble. Robbie tripped over Carry, Carry tripped over Leanne and Uncle Max pushed all of them out as fast as he could. They quickly regained their footing, though, and started moving fast, dodging soldiers trying to grab them like they had been born for it.

They managed to make it clear of the tents, but the number of people chasing them was only increasing. Max and Robbie had gotten ahead of the girls, but Leanne changed course without warning. Carry stumbled trying not to run into her, but she quickly caught back up. "Leanne! Where are you going? We have to get out of here!"

She pointed as they ran, and Carry's eyes widened as she realized what their new destination was.

Robbie and Max, meanwhile, had been the main targets for the soldiers, who had managed to outflank them. Before they could get away again, they realized they were surrounded. "You're not going any further," one of the soldiers gave them a nasty smile.

Carry and Leanne, forgotten for the moment, boarded the helicopter Leanne had seen currently sitting empty and unguarded.

"Keep your head down." Carry said as they ducked inside. "They'll never look for us in here. Good idea about a hiding spot"

"Hiding? I'm going to fly this thing." Leanne moved to the pilot's seat, starting to turn everything on.

"Wait. What?" Carry squeaked.

"Yeah, this is an AC-456 Bridgeport F class." Leanne was paying more attention to what she was doing than to Carry.

"So?" Carry was confused.

"Remember, the Island of Robot Monkeys? This is what I flew to get us out of the volcano."

"If you recall, I was blind from the laser rockets at the time," Carry noted.

"Oh yeah. Well, this is what I used. It's pretty simple to fly, actually." Leanne flipped a few more switches and the chopper came to life.

"How in the world did you learn all this?" Carry asked, sliding into the co-pilot seat.

"I had to learn pretty quickly. I kind made the rest up as I went along."

"Wait, so you flew us home in a chopper you didn't know how to fly?" Carry yelled in a whisper.

"I got the hang of it." She put on the flight helmet. "Please remain seated during our flight and keep your tray table and seat in the upright and locked position."

Carry raised an eyebrow. "In other words, strap in and hold on," Leanne said, flipping her visor down. The helicopter lifted off as the soldiers suddenly realized one of their own wasn't flying. The helicopter circled around to where Robbie and Max were being ordered to lay on the ground with their hands behind their head. A bright spotlight lit up the area, making everyone blink. "Step away from the prisoners." Carry's voice came over the speaker system.

The solder who had been getting ready to cuff Max and Robbie looked up. Once she was sure she had his attention, Leanne engaged the weapons system, with four rockets dropping down into launch position, aimed squarely at the group on the ground. After a long pause, the soldiers all laid their guns on the ground, putting their own hands behind their heads. Uncle Max and Robbie scrambled back to their feet and ran over to where Carry had dropped down a rope ladder. "Hurry up and get in!"

"Smell ya' later suckers!" Leanne shouted as both the boys scrambled on board and Leanne took them up and out of harm's way. They all got strapped into the seats, pulling on helmets of their own and making sure the communication system was up and running as Leanne got them out of the area.

"We need to move fast. I think I have a way to configure this Ruby into a mechanism that will let us contain the U.F.O. safely," Uncle Max said as soon as they were all online. "Head to my cabin in the Rockies."

Once they made it, Leanne carefully set the helicopter down in a clearing behind the cabin. She just hoped they had time to finish whatever they were doing here before someone flew overhead and noticed a large, stolen military-grade machine where one should not be.

Inside, they got a variety of snacks and headed down into the basement, where a state-of-the-art workshop and command center was hidden. "How can we stop this thing from freezing everything?" Carry asked.

Uncle Max walked over to table, placing both hands on the surface to activate sensors. A virtual keyboard appeared, and he quickly started inputting information. A box came out from the inside of the table, and he carefully put the ruby inside. Immediately information started scrolling across all the screens as the gem was analyzed down to its molecular structure.

"The Ruby is the most stable gem, right? That means it is Ai2o3, which means there's aluminum in its makeup. Aluminum doesn't freeze, so that must be the reason it wasn't effected." He paused, getting an odd look on his face. " Wait! Silk!"

Max spent several more minutes typing and muttering to himself as he ran more tests and scenarios. "Okay. I think I've got it!" He did a little dance.

Carry rolled her eyes at him. "Great – how?"

"So a diamond has a Mohs scale – which is used to measure the hardness of different minerals - of 10, and the ruby rates a 9. The aluminum ions replaced the chromium ions, and that's why rubies are red. There's more science to that, but that's the short version. What's important is that because of those properties, rubies were used to make the first lasers in the 1960s by Theodore Maiman. And I can use it to make a box to contain the UFO!"

Uncle Max raised the equipment and took out the ruby, holding it up to the light. He brought it to a laser cutter, carefully inputting the dimensions he would need. He stopped several times, measuring the air with his hands before glancing back at Carry. "You think the UFO was about this big?"

Carry shook her head. "I don't know."

Max made a face, continuing to try to estimate the size with his hands. "We can't make a mistake on this. If the ruby container is too small, it won't fit, but if we go too big we may not have enough ruby. I hope I am right."

He started typing again, but Carry suddenly shouted, making everyone jump. "Wait! I have an idea of how we can be sure!" She looked up to lights and stared at them for a moment. She thought back to the moment when she had seen the U.F.O. while they were on the base. She hadn't really paid attention at the time because there was so much happening, but she had seen the exact dimensions. She tried hard to picture exactly what she had seen as the numbers scrolled across her vision. The numbers hit her like a wave, making her stumble and fall to the floor.

"Carry! Are you okay?" Uncle Max rushed to her side.

"I know the answer." She beamed at him. "The length of the U.F.O. is one and three eighth inches. The Width is two and one eighth inches. And the height is three eighths of an inch!"

"Are you sure?" Uncle Max paused in his quest to look her over for injuries.

"Of course she's sure!" Robbie pumped his fist in the air. "My Math Glasses have been burned into her retinas. And you're welcome!"

Uncle Max rose and went to put the numbers into the computer. The machine came to life, and they watched as it cut the ruby into a box. It cut four sides, then the bottom, and then the top, and then used some of Max's special adhesive to connect it all together. It was the most expensive jewelry box ever made.

Max carefully picked it up and stowed it in his bag. "Lets go get us a U.F.O.!"

"Team Adventure Club Go!" Carry shouted putting her hand out. Robbie, Leanne and Max followed suit. "TEAM ADVENTURE CLUB!" they shouted.

"Well, this sounds like a cheer-leading club to me." Agent Coopee smirked.

They all whirled around to see him standing on the stairs. "Poop," Carry sighed.

"And what exactly are you up to down here? Very nice secret lair by the way."

Max was glad he had already stowed the box. "Well, we were hiding until you found us," he pointed out.

"You do realize the helicopter you stole has a GPS tracker on it," Agent Cooppee pointed out.

"Just bring them up here!" Agent Lasko's voice drifted down the stairs.

"You heard 'em. Move!"

The gang walk up the stairs with Uncle Max bringing up the rear. In the living room, four soldiers dressed in black stood with guns pointed at them.

"You can't keep us here. We're children! You have to be violating some mandate or law or something!" Carry pointed out.

Agent Cooppee grabbed her by the chin and started to squeeze. "You've got a big mouth for such a small girl. If you don't want to end up with it broken you might want learn to keep it shut."

Uncle Max narrowed his eyes. "I warned you that if you touched or harmed any of these children I would retaliate. You've just crossed my line."

"What are you going to do about it?" Agent Cooppee mocked him, squeezing a little harder, making Carry whimper.

In one movement, Uncle Max spun around and picked up the nearest table lamp, smashing it across Agent Cooppee's head. He grabbed Carry and pushed her behind him where she would be safer. One of the soldiers started to bring his gun around, but Max kicked out, catching him across the stomach, then landing a right hook across his face. The then grabbed his arm and sung him around and down, the guy's head impacting the coffee table and knocking him out.

"Bolo's!" Leanne shouted. Robbie and Carry both reached into a pocket on their belts and pulled out a tube. They put one end on their TAC-COMM and loaded them like muskets from the civil war.

Uncle Max had been busy dealing with the rest of the soldiers. He pulled the only one still conscious to his feet, spinning him around and putting him in a head lock. "We are only trying to help!" he said as he slammed the guy to the floor.

"Then perhaps you should end this charade!" Agent Cooppee pulled out a gun of his own.

Robbie turned to fire, but Agent Lasko threw a vase at him, and knocked him out cold. Carry and Leanne were hitting the Agents with the bolos. It wrapped them both up like turkies, forcing their arms and legs tightly to their bodies.

"Son of a..." Agent Cooppee swore as he dropped the gun and tumbled to the floor.

The cabin door flung open to reveal Sir Oliver Hedgestone. He was looking less frozen and more put-together than the last time they had seen him, but it was pretty obvious he was very, very angry.

"Give me the ruby!" His voice hadn't raised, but it sent chills up everyone's spines.

Max patted himself and looked confused. "What ruby? I haven't seen any ruby?"

"This is not a game you wish to play. Hand it over, or you and these... children... will find yourselves in very, shall we say unpleasant, circumstances."

Max glanced at Carry, trying to will her to run. But Carry wasn't going anywhere. She knew if she left and something happened, she would never forgive herself. After a moment, she suddenly burst into tears. "Stop I just want to go home!"

It was a little over-dramatic, she could admit, but it was effective. Sir Oliver Hedgestone actually looked startled. Leanne was kneeling next to Robbie, trying to get him to wake up. She caught Carry's eye and realized what was going on. She put both hands over her face and started to sob.

Sir Oliver Hedgestone took a deep breath before pulling out a small gun, pointing it right at Uncle Max. "Give me the ruby or your dear uncle is going to suffer."

They stopped crying and gave him identical hard looks. "Don't you do anything stupid, baldy," Leanne warned.

"Give me the ruby, and I'll be on my way. You and the military can work out your... issues... without my interference."

Uncle Max had absently scraped the dust from the cutting into his pocket earlier, and now he got as much of a handful as he could. When his attention was on Carry, Max tossed the ruby dust directly into Sir Oliver Hedgestone's face. The powder shimmered like a beautiful water fall of red, making him back up suddenly and drop the gun.

"My eyes!" Sir Oliver Hedgestone screamed.

"Run!" Uncle Max yelled, grabbing Robbie from the floor as he went past.

They ran back to the helicopter they had stolen, throwing on helmets as Leanne got the motors started back up.

"GO! GO! GO!"

Leanne did just that. Pulling back on the joystick, the helicopter lifted off the ground and into the air. High into the air.

20

CHAPTER 20

The whirling of the blades was creating a wonderful breeze across Robbie's face as he laid across the bench across from Uncle Max. He imagined that he was in a field somewhere enjoying the day. He could hear laughter in the distance, and he thought of hot dogs and cotton candy. Then he opened his eyes and sighed.

"You okay?" Uncle Max asked.

Robbie looked out over the dark forest with city lights winking in the distance. Inside, Leanne was piloting and Carry was busy on her TAC-COMM, while Uncle Max's hair was just blowing around like seaweed in the air. Not the same at all.

"Robbie?" Uncle Max repeated.

He gave a weak smile. "I'm fine. My head just hurts."

"That's because it was hit with a three hundred year old vase. A one of a kind relic. A priceless piece of ancient Egyptian artifact. But you know, whatever," Uncle Max patted his shoulder gingerly.

"Well, as long as I'm fine right?" Robbie managed a grin.

"Oh, yeah. Much better."

Robbie squinted at him.

"It was three hundred years old Robbie!" Uncle Max yelled.

"I didn't smash it with my face on purpose!"

They were interrupted by Carry, who had been plotting their course. "These coordinates say we're only about a minute away from the GAST Center."

"GAST Center?" Robbie blinked, dragging his mind back on target.

"The Galactic Assembly for Science and Technology Center, our next detination." Uncle Max rubbed a hand across his face.

Leanne landed them in an open field that contained only a small concrete door in the ground in the center. "Is that it?"

Uncle Max turn putting half his body out of the wide opening of the helicopter looking down to the field.

"That's it!" Uncle Max hopped out, the ground squelching up around him. The mud was up past his ankles. He picked up one foot and gave it a horrified stare.

Robbie, Leanne and Carry followed, all finding themselves in mud up to their knees. Carry looked as disgusted as Uncle Max and Robbie just shrugged it off, but Leanne started grinning. "Now, this is an adventure!"

At the door, Uncle Max pulled out a large key. It was metal, long and square. In the center there were two blue lights and the top was a thumb print identifier. When Max put the key in the lock the lights turned green and the scanner verified his identity.

"Why are we here?" Robbie had leaned forward to watch with interest.

"We need the largest magnifying glass known to man," Uncle Max grunted as he pulled the heavy door open.

Inside, the corridor flickered its lights on as they walked down the narrow concrete structure. From the other side, lights started to flicker on as someone came to greet them. As they approached it was easy to make out that one of them was a scientist, with three guards flanking her. Uncle Max put his hand out to shake but she smacked her hand across his face instead.

"I haven't heard from you in three months!" She seemed shaken, but quickly regained her composure. "And who are these little darlings?"

"Hello Isabelle." Max said rubbing his face. "This is my niece Carry, and her friends Leanne and Robbie."

"Why on earth have you brought children to GAST Center?" Isabelle was talking through her teeth, her smile brittle.

"We need the YOLO Telescope."

She raised an eyebrow. "Why? Are you showing them the surface of Jupiter?"

"No, no. I meant we need to reposition it to Earth, to Belleview Heights specifically. I'll fill you in on the way" Max said.

They continued down the corridor to yet another large metal door. Isabelle ushered them inside, and as they entered the building all three kids stopped and stared. It was huge. Carry couldn't imagine that all of this was underground. The whole place looked like a control room for NASA with tons of scientists walking around in lab coats and other people in suits and ties or dress skirts and jackets. And it seemed like everyone knew Uncle Max.

Isabelle grabbed Max, pulling him aside. "Why haven't you called me?"

"I was working. I just got back a few days ago only to have my entire home town frozen solid," he sighed softly.

"You don't think we're not aware of the projectile that froze your town?" Isabelle asked. She pressed a button, and the monitors all switched to show their town.

Carry watched the soldiers still trying to figure out ways to pick up the UFO, while others showed different views of the camp, and the soldiers going about their business. Carry spotted caravan of SUVs pulling up and Sir Oliver Hedgestone exiting one of them, looking worse for wear, but still elegant and angry. "Uh, guys?"

Everyone came over to look, and Isabelle pressed a few buttons, the screen zooming in, and then analyzing his face. A moment later, a full bio appeared, following him as he walked into the camp. "That is Sir Oliver Hedgestone, a billionaire, explorer and extortion master. He's ruthless, and will stop at nothing until he has everything he wants."

"Oh we know him!" Carry made a face.

"You do?"

"Yeah, we've met him a few times, but we've never been properly introduced. I think Uncle Max may have blinded him." Carry said.

"How?" Isabelle glanced over at Max, who was trying to look innocent.

"Ruby dust." Carry beamed.

"Just be careful and don't cross him. He's bad news, and you don't need him as an enemy." Isabelle glanced back at the screen, shaking her head.

After a pause where they all just watched the screen, thinking, Uncle Max clapped his hands, making everyone jump. "Okay. Let's get me to the YOLO telescope."

"You can't just go to the Yellers Outer-space Light Observer Telescope Max," Isabelle looked cross again. "Not without proper clearance."

Max pulled out an ID card that stated he has clearance for all levels of classification. Isabelle looked at it for a long moment before handing it back. She shook her head, but it was obvious she was admitting defeat. "Okay then. Let's go."

21

CHAPTER 21

The doctors laid Sir Oliver Hedgestone on an operating table. He didn't look good. The ruby dust was damaging his eyes and the doctors wanted to get it out as fast as they could. It was going to be a long process.

Outside, Colonel Roberts was furious. "You mind explaining why several military personnel and AIA Agents are chasing a bunch of twelve years around the state?"

"They are wanted fugitives from the Military, Sir." Sergeant Collins refused to back down.

"What on earth could three twelve year olds have done to make two of the country's top agents get in the most expensive helicopters we own and try and shoot them out of the sky?"

"Sir. We were after Maximilian Bonnefield." Sergeant Collins pointed out.

Colonel Roberts gave him a hard look before turning to Agents Cooppee and Lasko. "And you two. What are you up to?"

"We are under orders to only speak to Sir Oliver Hedgestone. Sir." Agent Cooppee sneered.

Colonel Roberts never took his eyes off them as he pointed to Sergeant Collins. "Arrest this man."

Several Military Police standing nearby moved in, quickly handcuffing the officer. "Why are you arresting me?" Sergeant Collins sputtered.

"For plotting to kill children." Colonel Roberts watched as both agents showed flickers of surprise before their expressions went blank again. "As for you two. I'm watching."

Colonel Roberts and Secret Inspector Bonnefield, who had stood by watching silently, both gave the agents another hard look before they headed toward the command tent. Agents Cooppee and Lasko just looked at each other and smiled.

Colonel Roberts and Secret Inspector Bonnefield walked past the field where soldiers were still freezing themselves. "Someone tell those men to stop trying to pick it up. Look at the fifty other soldiers who are frozen solid – they are not going to succeed." Secret Inspector Bonnefield ordered a passing soldier. He changed direction to go take care of the problem, while Colonel Roberts continued to escort their prisoner.

Inside the tent, Sergeant Collins had his handcuffs removed. "You think they bought the bait?" Colonel Roberts sat down in one of the chairs.

"I hope so. What kind of mad man puts out a hit on twelve year olds?" Sergeant Collins took another chair, rubbing at his wrists. "So we just wait."

"It must have been tempting to go through with taking the deal, knowing your son could have gone to Harvard." Colonel Roberts pushed an open laptop over, giving the sergeant access to their current information.

"None at all. I explained it to my son, and he and I agreed it wasn't worth the stress of knowing that his only reason for being in school was because I had harmed anyone. Children or otherwise."

"Admirable." Colonel Roberts smiled.

The medical tent was in full swing as the doctors removed the ruby dust from Sir Oliver Hedgestone's eyes. It was a difficult long process, but they finally had to call it. "Okay, wrap up his eyes. I think I've done all I can. We need to Aeroflight him to the nearest hospital. They might be able to do more there." The doctor in charge set down his instruments, looking tired as the nurses jumped into action, preparing the patient and calling for the medical evac.

Agents Lasko and Cooppee watched as the medical helicopter was loaded and quickly flew away. They both straightened their ties and started making their way to a nearby black SUV. As they approached, several MP's stepped out followed by Secret Inspector Bonnefield. "Agents." He gave them both a humorless smile. "Soldiers, arrest these men."

"Arrest us? We are AIA Agents." Agent Lasko stood up straighter. "You can't arrest us. We are a branch of the government that answers only to the Executive Administrator for the agency."

"Have you ever met the Executive Administrator of the AIA?" Secret Inspector Bonnefield raised an eyebrow at them.

"No." Agent Lasko said, but was cut off before he could say anything more.

"Well, now you can say you have had that pleasure." Secret Inspector Bonnefield said, bowing slightly. He pulled out a silver and gold badge featuring an eagle with spread wings in front of a circular flying saucer and a sunburst. A banner underneath read *"The Stars are just the Beginning"* in bold Greek lettering.

After a long moment where both agents lost most of the color in their faces, they both stuck out their hands and the MP's promptly place handcuffs on both the men. "We were just following orders," Agent Lasko said.

"Yes. From an unsanctioned and non-liable billionaire who, need I mention, is a civilian and in no way part of our chain of command." Secret Inspector Bonnefield glared at them. "Get them out of my sight."

22

CHAPTER 22

Carry, Leanne, and Robbie were in awe as they stepped into one of the biggest rooms they had ever been in. It was currently housing several space shuttles that were sleeker and more futuristic looking than anything NASA used.

"These are space ships?" Carry asked in a whisper, afraid to raise her voice.

"Yes." Isabelle said, smiling. "But these are so much better. Come on." Isabelle ushered them further down the catwalk to an open service elevator.

Robbie couldn't stop staring at the shuttles. He wanted to go inside one. He wanted to ride one. Leanne reached over, grabbing Robbie's hand as the elevator shifted and started descending down the four stories to a docking bay floor. Robbie looked at her hand and didn't know how to react. Was she just scared or was there something more to this? He decided to just let his hand stay there and turned his attention back to the shuttles.

As they exited the elevator, they were met by a large, muscular man. He was also wearing a lab coat, but he looked different. For one, he was wearing jeans and sneakers, and on his sneakers were roller skate attachments. He had a huge Afro and was wearing frosted eyeglasses. Isabelle rolled her eyes at him. "This is Doctor Rafael Williams, our professor of trans-orbital rotation and engineering."

He rolled up, spinning in a circle and giving Max a high five. "Maximilian my man! Heard you was in Mexico dealing with some Aztec gold."

"I was. But it's all good now." Max said, going into a complicated handshake with a lot of wiggling and slapping.

"And who are these fine looking kids?" Rafael held up a hand for Robbie, who enthusiastically high-fived him as well.

"We're Team Adventure Club!" Carry said proudly.

"I'll be! The Team Adventure Club? Consider me your biggest fan." He gave them all a huge thumbs up with both hands. "Call me Rafa."

They all introduced themselves, and Rafa shook his head. "Crazy stuff man. You kids are wild. Gotta watch out for my job!" He grinned at them. "So, what brings you all here to this fine establishment?"

Max pointed to the middle shuttle. Rafa looked, then spun on his skates a few times. "You want the KRS-1?"

"I need to get to the YOLO and reposition it toward earth."

Rafa looked at them for a moment before nodding. "Chance to be part of a TAC mission? Count me in. Let's do this."

Rafa led them to a locker room. On the walls there were space suits hanging in a wide range of colors and patterns. Leanne was immediately drawn to the Black ones. "These are the coolest!"

Carry ran her hand over one of the suits, and the material felt strange; it was rubbery and soft but hard at the same time. The elbows and knees had padding already in place, and the shoulders looked as if there was a hard plastic over them. There was a small GAST logo on the right chest and a NASA logo on the left chest. The back of the suits had a carbon metal running down the center of the spine, and there were two straps that wrapped around to the front of the suit connecting the back spine piece to the front chest piece.

They continued past the suits and through a weight room with Astronauts running on treadmills and lifting weights. Through a window, Carry watched as one of them spared with what she thought was a human - until he kicked its head off. Carry looked at Robbie with surprised glee. "They have robots!"

"I know! Did you see how he kicked its head off?" Robbie was vibrating with excitement.

Uncle Max leaned in patting them each on the shoulder. "You haven't seen anything yet."

23

CHAPTER 23

The suit was a little small on Uncle Max. He danced around, wiggling his fat into place until he was finally able to zip it up. It made him look skinner, he thought, and he admired himself in the full length mirror. He was proud to be in a flight suit again. It had been far too long since his days in space.

Carry came around the corner, also in a space suit. Max grinned at her. "You look awesome!"

Carry's smile was quickly broken when Leanne walked in. She was furious that she wasn't going to get to go to space. Robbie was happy that he didn't have to leave the earth's atmosphere today. He wasn't big on heights, and leaving the earth was getting pretty high. Too high. Being able to see earth with his own eyes from space was the last thing in his book of *Things You Need to Do Before You Die.*

"I am so jealous that you get to go into space!" Leanne huffed.

"Leanne, we need you to fly the helicopter back to base so Robbie can grab the UFO and conceal it in the ruby box," Max patted her on the shoulder.

"I know. But...." She moaned, looking at Carry – and Carry's space suit – with puppy dog eyes.

"We better get going folks. You have thirty-two minutes to get to the space station and redirect toward Bellview Heights. After that you going to have to wait an entire day," Rafa said, skating in.

Uncle Max smiled at Carry. "Ready?"

The door to the main hangar opened, and they saw the giant ships once again. "Since we have to get you into space rather quickly, we'll take the middle one." Rafa smiled. "It's the fastest out of the three and should get us into space in about five minutes. We get to the station in twenty minutes, giving us twelve minutes to work on the positioning of the YOLO."

"Okay, Leanne, get Robbie to the UFO and get it in the box. Seal it up tight, and put it in another box. A wooden one and, latch that with a lock as well. You have 32 minutes to get back to Belleview Heights." Max put both hands on her shoulders, forcing her to refocus on her own task.

"Thirty-two minutes to go one hundred miles? That's a hundred and eighty-seven point five miles an hour. Most military helicopters can maintain an average speed of about two hundred miles an hour, so, we should be fine." She beamed at him.

"That's what I wanted to hear!" Uncle Max said, squeezing her shoulders before letting go. "No one else can fly a helicopter like you."

Leanne and Robbie watched as they loaded into the shuttle and the door was latched behind them. "We better move!" Robbie said.

The inside of the shuttle was beautiful. Max smiled as waves of memories washed over him. "Where do you want me," he asked Rafa.

"You can pilot, my good man. I'll navigate." Rafa smacked Max on the back, taking his own place.

Max sat down and smiled wide. He strapped himself in, adjusted the buckles and the steering column, and looked over the console before pressing a red button. It buzzed to life, revealing that the entire thing was touch screen. Rafa did the same, booting up the navigation console, and Carry took her seat behind them. As the ship whizzed to life the seat belts automatically readjusted, squeezing them in tight. Uncle Max grunted and exhaled. "They really want you to be safe, huh?"

He could feel the rumble of the engines through the seat. He loved the feeling of the ship coming to life, ready for its journey. He pressed several buttons on the monitor, watching as the giant bay doors opened. Then hydraulics pushed the Shuttle up to a forty-five degree angle.

Rafa finished programming their course, and grinned at Max. "Here we go!"

The shuttle blasted off so fast that before Carry knew it they were thirty thousand feet in the air. She could see out the front window, but all she could see was clouds whizzing by. The shuttle was flying straight and quiet. She looked at the altimeter in the center of the console and it already said they were at fifty-one thousand feet. Her eyes got wide - they were outside the Earth's atmosphere. She could see stars. She was amazed at how beautiful it was. She was totally in awe of the universe.

"Cool isn't it?" Uncle Max asked.

Carry couldn't find words. She just nodded with a wide grin and the look of wonder in her eyes. She could see the moon. It was so bright as it just floated there. The Sun was way far away, but she could see that too. Carry raised her TAC-COM towards the front window and snapped a few pictures. She couldn't wait to show Leanne and Robbie. She started doing a little dance in her seat. Then she notice that both Rafa and Uncle Max were also dancing in their seats.

"Woot! Woot! We're in space! We're in space!" they all sang.

Meanwhile, Leanne was pushing her helicopter to its limits. They were flying so fast and so low that Robbie was just watching things pass by. He tapped on his TAC-COM and It buzzed to life. "Another eight minutes and we'll be there!"

"Good. I can't wait for this night to be over!" Leanne sulked.

"What's wrong with you?" Robbie asked.

"I just...Ahhh...It's not fair. I'm the pilot! I'm the one who should have gone to space! Carry doesn't even want to be an astronaut. I do! She's a geologist! Not a pilot! I'm the one who should be in space right now," Leanne wailed.

"But you're pushing the very limits with one of the government's super secret helicopters!" Robbie pointed out.

"I know. I get it. But... It's just not fair!"

"Six minutes," Robbie said.

"Are you even listening to me?"

Robbie rolled his eyes, sorry he had brought it up, but he nodded.

"I love her Robbie, but sometimes...I mean...graaaah. Right?" She was gesturing wildly as she complained.

"Both hands on the controls there Missy!" Robbie grabbed his seat, going a little white.

"I'm not going to crash us. If I can't go to space, I'm going to break speed records! You can bank on it," she shouted.

24

CHAPTER 24

The shuttle coasted through space silently. Every once in a while, a thruster would hiss out a long extended boost of fusion. The ship seemed so tiny against the backdrop of the vast universe. The stars reflected off the metal exterior and it was almost as if the ship got lost in the blanket of the cosmos.

"We're about three minutes out," Rafa said, looking back to Carry. "Once we dock with the space station, Harry will meet us. He's already calculated the trajectory of the angle in which we'll need to position the telescope. Max, it's up to you replace the lens."

"Carry and I can space-walk out to the front of the telescope." Max said tapping the console.

"Wait. Space walk?" Carry blinked.

"Yes. We have to go out to the telescope and flip the lens so it magnifies the sun's heat. It should take but a moment," Max shot a mile back to her.

Carry gripped the armrests until her knuckles turned white. Going into space was neat, but a space walk?. Maybe Leanne should have come instead.

As they rose over the space station on approach she saw a strange space ship docked on the other side. It was red and yellow, and looked old and beaten, with strange markings she didn't recognize. "Earth Shuttle regulated to docking station three," a voice said over the speaker.

"Shuttle bay three heard. Making changes on coordinates," Rafa replied.

The ship rose up and then shifted hard right and seemingly upside down. It made Carry disoriented, and she had to close her eyes. The shuttle lined up along the docking platform, and huge magnets fitted themselves against ship, locking it into place along the walkway. It reminded Carry being on a plane when it would taxi into the terminal. Except in space, which was cooler.

Both Max and Rafa flipped switches above their heads and then raised their hands as to not touch anything. Carry watched as the console flashed and buzzed with symbols and numbers.

"There's nothing to worry about, Carry, the space station has an automatic dock protocol. We just let the station do all the work, Max glanced back, catching the worried look on her face.

"What is that ship?" she asked, pointing to the one she had seen coming in.

"Oh, that's a Bogarian Ship from the Eagle Nebula. They are like the police of the universe," Max reassured her. "They look like warthogs and can be very brutal if you break a space law, but no need to worry. Earth has a sanction with them for the Milky Way Galaxy."," he continued.

"So aliens really do exist?" Carry asked.

"Oh yes, far more then you can imagine. There are millions of aliens. We are aliens too, to every other race," he noted.

"But... We're not aliens. We're from Earth..." Carry rubbed at her head, trying to push away the headache building.

"Which is just one of billions of planets. Earth is just the one of the smaller ones that still believes it's alone in the universe," Max said.

Carry looked away. He was right. All this time she thought they were alone in the universe, and therefore all other species were aliens. But earth is just another planet. Earthlings are aliens to everyone else. She smiled as she thought about all the different species that must be out there. "How many alien races have you met Uncle Max?"

"Seven," he grinned back at her.

The ship buzzed and chirped again. "*Docking completed.*" The ship rocked a little more and then stopped. They all got up and headed back to the door, where Rafa released the seal, letting in a loud hiss of air as the pressure equalized. On the other side of the door was Harry, a Borgarian. He was only about five feet tall, but he was thick with muscle. Max was right — he looked just like a warthog wearing cool armor and a helmet. He made a loud grunt and breathed out of his large nostrils. Then he laughed.

Max and Harry immediately embraced each other. The little alien picked up Max like he didn't weigh a thing. "Maximilian! It has been far too long for us not to have seen each other! I have missed you, my friend"

"Harry great to see you! Meet my niece, Carry," Max reached around and pulled a wide-eyed Carry forward.

"Niece?" Harry asked.

"My sister's child. We call them niece for girls and nephews for boys." Max said.

"Ah!" Harry said. "We have the same on Bogar. But we say Chutee and Nuntee."

"Hello Mr. Harry," Carry felt very shy, and wanted to hide behind Max, but she gathered up her courage and smiled at him.

"The pleasure is mine, niece of Maximilian. You shall be my Chutee as well!" He pulled her in for a hug too. She stiffened, then relaxed, giggling. She was now considered a family member to alien species! How cool was that!

Harry moved on to Rafa next, exchanging more hugs. "Harry, you look healthy as ever!"

"You flatter me. I am old and sore," Harry made a face.

"Oh, that's right. Your birthday was two months ago! I'm sorry I missed it." Rafa said as they started walking into the station.

"Graah, you didn't miss anything. It was a thousand of my in-laws, and Brathu's mother was in rare form. Just what I needed to bring in my hundred and seventh birthday."

"Did you say you are a hundred and seven years old?" Carry didn't mean to interrupt, but she couldn't help it.

"Don't remind me," Harry grunted as he waved a security card in front of a pad, opening a door.

"Is that old or young for a Bogarian?" Now that she had gotten past the surprise, she wanted to know everything.

"Well, I'm technically still young. My father is eleven hundred years old."

"Eleven hundred?!" Carry stopped dead in her tracks. The men all chuckled and got her moving again.

They walked through a large control room where a few different alien races were working on computers, along with a several humans. The Bogarians were the only ones armed with weapons, and they stood by doors and a few patrolled the hallways. They finally came to what looked like a large, empty airplane hangar, with a helmets and air tanks on the wall. "This is the walk room," Max said as they headed down to the equipment.

Carry watched Harry put the helmet on Max and how he connected the breathing tubes to the belted apparatus behind him. The two tubes went in with the red tips to the belt, and the blue tips to the oxygen tanks. Then Harry spun a strange circular tube and a small thruster popped out on both sides of Max's tanks. "Remember how to use your jets?" he asked.

"Huh, you invented these things?" Max laughed.

"Some fat earthling did, if I recall correctly." Harry replied, making Rafa laugh.

"You call it fat, I call it love jiggles." Max did a little dance, making his gut move around.

Still laughing, Harry led Rafa and Carry out of the room. "Once they open these doors, we'd be sucked out," he explained to Carry.

Max attached a clamp to a metal ring on his belt. The clamp was connected to a cable on a reel attached to the wall. He walked up to two glowing foot pads in the center of the room as they filed out. Carry and Rafa went into the observation room. They could see everything on a flat screen monitor the size of a truck. The huge bay doors opened, and the blue lights on the foot pads turned green. Max leaped up like Superman. Carry watched with wide eyes.

Max reached the end of the cable and floated in space for a moment before unbuckling his clamp and using his thrusters to maneuver to the large telescope. "Almost there," He said into his microphone.

"You're doing great," Harry encouraged.

Carry turned around to see him sitting at a monitoring station. She walked over so she could see everything from Max's point of view. The telescope look so much bigger this way. Max was getting closer when Carry noticed something moved off to the left of the screen.

"Uncle Max did you see that?" she asked.

"See what?"

"Something moved on the telescope."

Max looked around but didn't see anything. Until a laser shot past him, followed by several more. Max moved quickly, using his thrusters to spiral toward the telescope as he dodged more blasts.

"All units! Agent under attack!. Unknown aggressors. All units respond. Human species in space walk. Use caution." Harry was yelling over the intercom.

Sirens started walling, and several Bogarian police units moved quickly. They were outside the space station in seconds. Carry watched about thirty of them jetting into space with laser rifles ready. They were leaping off the sides of the space station like frogs while using their thruster packs to navigate toward the telescope.

25

CHAPTER 25

Leanne pushed the helicopter to its limits as she pulled it up over the last group of trees. She could see the military camp in the distance, and lights flickered against the frozen town. She looked at her TAC-COM. They had eight minutes left as long as things continued to go as planned. They would be fine. She looked to the sky wishing she could see what Max and Carry were doing, but all she could see was a strange light show. "What do you think that's all about?"

Robbie moved up so he could see the red lights flashing. It looked almost like one light going back and forth, but Robbie knew better. He'd seen laser fights before. Mostly on his favorite movie, Robo-Police Ultra Ninja Force, but it was still valid experience. He looked at Leanne with a lump in his throat. "It's not good."

"Then we need to get this job done and ASAP."

As they got closer, the console started to beep with red lights. Then a monitor blinked and showed several incoming homing rockets. Leanne didn't say anything, but she reached up and pulled her seat belt latches tighter. Robbie sat back down and did the same.

She raised them higher into the sky before pushing a few buttons causing a burst of fiery debris to launch out from underneath the helicopter. She then pulled hard to the right and went almost completely sideways. The helicopter made a tight turn on its side before she pushed the joystick down hard and had them almost pointed straight down toward the ground.

Robbie was busy working on his TAC-COM. He placed a grappling hook in the end and programmed in his math. "Just get me over the alien missile, I'll do the rest."

"It's a hot zone, so I can't land. You'll have to grab it on the fly!" The helicopter leveled out over a small section of houses and flew quickly past the neighborhood at top speed. Three helicopters were still in hot pursuit.

"I don't need you to land. I do need your TAC-COM though," he shouted.

"What? Why?"

"Just give it to me."

Leanne quickly pushed a button on the bottom of her TAC-COM, releasing it from her wrist. She felt weird not having it on. She hasn't taken it off in two years. She handed it to Robbie. "You break that and I'll kill you!"

"Yeah, yeah." Robbie put her communicator on his other hand, loading it with a grappling hook as well.

"What are you going to do?" Leanne asked as she pushed the joystick all the way to the left making the helicopter turn almost sideways again as a rocket went sailing underneath them.

"I have an idea. Just get me close."

He made his way to the gunner seat and leaned far out of the helicopter. Everything slowed down as he watched a rocket burn past them with only inches to spare. But he just focused on that alien missile sitting in the frozen field.

Leanne pulled the joystick to the right, making the helicopter turn wide. "I'll circle around and fly straight up from the ball field," she shouted back to him.

Robbie was waiting until they were in a range. He had no idea what he was going to do, but he knew he had to get that missile into the ruby box, no matter what. As they shot past the baseball field, he got an idea. "Get low to the ground. I'm going to water ski!"

Leanne glanced back. "What? Really?"

He nodded.

"You got it. You know if you hit any of those frozen soldiers you're going to splat like spaghetti right," she asked.

"Oh yeah, if that happens, I'm toast. I won't hit them."

Leanne dropped the helicopter to almost ten feet off the ground. Robbie stepped out onto the landing rail holding onto the inside of the helicopter. He leaned out, getting ready. "Wanna slow it down a little?"

"I did. We're only going a hundred and fifty," she hollered back.

"Oh, well then," he rubbed a hand across his face. "Here goes nothing!"

Robbie leapt out, raising his left arm toward the helicopter. He fired the TAC-COM, and the grappling hook slammed into the side, the cable spiraling out with a whizzing sound. Robbie dangled behind the helicopter just off the ground. He tried to gently touch his feet to the ice, but the speed knocked him up and almost into the helicopter blade. He reeled himself in a little and tried again. His feet tapped the ice, and he bounced again, but not as high. He looked down to see a rocket shoot past him and explode into the ground. "What is wrong with these idiots?!"

Robbie dropped again, putting his feet to the ice one more time, and this time it worked. He was skiing behind the helicopter.

"We are three hundred yards out from the object!" Leanne said over the microphone in the helmet.

Robbie reeled in the cable a little, but bullets started piercing the ice in front him. Great, now he had to dodge bullets too.

Leanne looked at the button for the machine gun and still didn't want to push it. She would feel really bad if anyone was hurt because of her. But they were being pushed to the limit with rockets being fired at them and now machine guns. She looked out to see Robbie skiing across the ice and dodging bullets. She didn't know what to do. They were in far over their heads. They were literally about to open fire on the military.

Then she saw another helicopter engaging the others. "I'm going to clear you a path!" Sergeant Collins said over the mic. "You get to the object! I got your back, Team Adventure Club!"

Leanne watched as two helicopters exploded. She slowed them down a little, and Robbie released the cable. Now he was in free mode. He was on his own. He skated down the ice at a hundred miles an hour. He pulled his knees in and lowered himself, keeping focused on his objective. He could see it now. He shot the grappling hook into the ice and used it to slow him down a little. He dropped to his side and slid feet first at it. He pulled the box out before releasing the grappling hook and letting it reel itself back into his TAC-COM. He slid to the UFO with the box out and opened, slamming into it and capturing the object inside before slamming the lid shut.

Leanne looked down to see the missile, but it was gone. Robbie had done it! She cheered before realizing he was still going. She knew he wasn't going to stop unless he hit something, so she had to catch him. She sped up again and was just about to reach him when the console alerted her to another incoming missile.

She had to move quickly. She pushed the joystick left and down. The helicopter dove straight down, almost spinning completely on its nose on the frozen ground. The rocket hit the earth behind her and exploded, damaging the tail rotors. The helicopter lifted up and was immediately out of control. The helicopter was in a spin and headed right for Robbie.

Robbie immediately thought the worst. As the helicopter spun past him he could see Leanne trying to steer it. With his right hand he shot his TAC-COM at the frozen ground and he aimed Leanne's at her. He waited for the right moment and fired. The grappling hook shot through the air and right at Leanne. She saw it coming, and unsnapped her seat belt as it smashed through the windshield. She grabbed it and was lifted out of her seat as the helicopter spun her out of the windshield.

She had landed perfectly. The helicopter spun recklessly, crashing and exploding behind her. However Robbie was still sliding. She slammed the prongs of her grappling hook into the ice. Robbie was pushing it to its limits as it started to smoke, but he was decelerating. Then his TAC-COM snapped and shattered off his wrist. It was up to Leanne's now. He hoped it would hold him, but the cable snapped hard and slung him into a wide arc as he circled back toward Leanne. As he slid past, he tossed the box in her direction. "Take it!"

The box slid to Leanne, and she scooped it up. She put it in her pocket as Sergeant Collins landed in front of her. The propellers whirred to a stop as he got out and saluted her.

"Good job soldier!"

"Thanks for saving my life," she grinned at him.

"I missed one." Sergeant Collins pointed at Robbie was making a habit of sliding all over the place now.

She watched him for a moment. "Well, we're alive."

"What about him?"

"I imagine he'll stop at some point right?" She shrugged.

26

CHAPTER 26

Max was using part of the metal structure pf the telescope for cover. The lasers slammed into it, each one melting it a little more. "Any clue as to who is attacking us?" Harry's voice crackled over the microphone.

"The same ones responsible for the freeze missile on Earth. The Orthonians. They want our planet to become a frozen tundra so they can take over." Max said, leaning out and firing his TAC-COM laser at them. He hit one, sending it spinning out into space.

Carry watched as the battle continued. "Uncle Max be careful!"

Max made his way around the telescope, landing on a flat surface. He clicked a knob on his boots, magnetizing them. He ran to meet up with two Bogarians who were returning fire. He stuck his hand out, and one of them tossed a laser rifle to him. He held it for a moment. The weight was familiar. He knew this weapon well. But it seemed like a life time ago. Almost as if he lived another life entirely. He was sick of the fighting.

Max reached down, clicking his boots again before leaping back into the air. He fired, hitting another Orthonian before coming under major fire again. He pushed himself off another beam that was nearby, reaching another platform and ducking back into cover.

"We have five minutes Max. I just got word from Earth. They have isolated the missile, and it is secure," Rafa said.

"I'm pinned down!" Max shouted.

Carry didn't hesitate. She ran back to the jump room, quickly putting on a helmet and slinging on an oxygen tank and thruster pack. She ran to the foot launch pads, and they lit up. The computer started to speak over the intercom: "*Launching in five. Four. Three. Two. One.*"

Rafa looked at Harry. "What's launching in five?" He looked down at his monitors and gasped. Rafa ran to the bay door, looking through the window, but it was too late. The room had already been pressurized, and he couldn't stop it. "Carry! No!" He watched as she launched into space. Without a secure cable.

Carry launched into space at full speed. She had her hands down by her sides and on her thrusters. She was steering her self with the thrusters at full speed. She looked at the telescope and all the Bogarians and Orthoninas. She closed her eyes and squeezed them hard. There was a white flash. As she opened her eyes she could see her trajectory path laid out before her. Robbie's mistake with the glasses was paying off. She guided herself though impossible openings, and she arced herself high above the battle and through space. Her first objective was to take out the Orthonians. She shot past a Bogarian. "Toss me a rifle!"

The Bogarian flung his weapon at her, and she turned back around, flying sideways. She lined up her gun and shot an Orthonian in the foot, knocking him off the telescope. This freed up Max who was able to start moving up to the lens. Carry just kept circling the platform, knocking Orthonians off one at a time while avoiding every attempt to take her out.

Max reached the top of the telescope where an Orthonian was waiting. It aimed its gun at Max. "Give up Earth hero!"

"Never." Max smacked the gun out of the small alien's hand. He then slammed its head against a metal rung, knocking it out and then stuffing into a small space for retrieval later. He used his access card to open the door to the lens controls.

"Two minutes Max!" Rafa shouted.

Max was inside the telescope now. It was small and cramped. He opened a console and put in the coordinates to Belleview Heights. The telescope rotated away from the sun and toward earth. He continued to input the commands, ignoring the warnings popping up that what he was doing was considered dangerous. He heard Carry come to land nearby, and he heard her fending off more aliens, but he had to stay focused.

"Forty-five seconds, Max."

Max input the last few numbers and the telescope aligned with the sun. A beam of light shot through the telescope, lighting up the inside. The word "*SUCCESSFUL*" blinked on the monitor. Carry and Max laughed andhugged each other.

They could hear the whole space station clapping through their headphones. "C'mon, let's get back."

Leanne and Sergeant Collins were still standing in the field when a wave of warm sunlight washed over them. They stand there for a moment to bask in the warmth. Leanne looked up, grinning. "They did it!"

Sergeant Collins tilted his head in question.

"Carry and Uncle Max. They went to space to align the YOLO Telescope so the sun could melt the town," she explained.

"That's... really?"

"Yeah. That's the kind of stuff we do," she beamed proudly.

"You mean besides fly military-grade helicopters and have dog fights in the air?"

"Well, that too. But mostly we save the day."

"We?" Sergeant Collins asked.

"Yeah, Team Adventure Club!"

"Team Adventure Club? I like it!" He gave her a salute, grinning as the grass around them all started to melt.

Robbie was seriously getting bored of sliding on ice now. He could feel the ice melting under him, turning the ground to mud, and finally allowing him to stop. He tried to stand up, but he was extremely dizzy at this point. After several attempts to get to his feet, he gave up in frustration. Leanne walked over and plopped down into the mud with him, slinging an arm around his shoulders. "You got style Robbie, even if you don't always know what you're doing."

"And you're not a bad pilot, if I do say so myself," He leaned over and planted a kiss on her cheek.

Leanne turned pink, but she smiled and looked away in time to see two military men walking over. She recognized Secret Inspector Bonnefield.

"Leanne, I trust you have the box in safe custody," he asked.

She nodded, handing over the box. "Amazing job kids! I am more than proud of you."

"No matter what you do, never open it," Leanne said.

He chuckled, but nodded. "You don't have to worry about that!"

"What a night!" Robbie said.

"I just want to go to bed," Leanne let out a breath.

They laid back in the mud and watched as two figures jumped out of a shuttle as it went past, and floated down to them. They got to their feet while Leanne helped to steady Robbie and then rushed over to where the others landed. "You guys did it!"

"Us?! You managed to get the UFO into the ruby box!" Max scooped them all up in big hugs.

"That was all Robbie!" Leanne bounced on her toes.

"Me!? You took out thirty helicopters. You should have seen it!" Robbie shouted.

"We fought aliens in a laser fight!" Carry was practically vibrating.

"Aliens?" Robbie's eyes went wide.

"Yeah, like real aliens. I met two different races. Some of them were the ones trying to take over the Earth, but the other one was awesome. He looked like a warthog! He was named Harry."

"I'm just glad you're safe!" Leanne hugged her best friend hard.

"So, who wants to do it again?" Max asked.

They all looked in different directions before cracking up.

As the sun rose for the day, the telescope heated the ice, thawing out the town and sending icy cold water rushing out of town toward the beach. Everyone was confused and wet.

Malcom, Robbie's best friend, was still sitting at his computer staring at his homework. He jumped when the ice thawed him, and his electronics came back to life. Until his computer sparked and went black. "What? No. No. No. My homework!" Then he looked around and saw that everything was wet. "Wait, why is everything all wet?"

And poor Miss Tinderam's dog finally made it back home. It was cold, shivering and soaking wet. Miss Tinderam found her poor little baby on the front porch, and picked it up, squeezing it so hard it looked as if its eyes were going to burst right out of its head. He just licked her in return.

Sadly no one will ever know what happened that night. No one remembered what happened, and not a soul will ever know that Team Adventure Club saved their seaside town. Everyone will go about their business as usual, going to work, going to school, having fun at the beach and playing in the parks. Because the world isn't ready for people like Carry, Leanne, Robbie and Uncle Max. They are a new breed of heroes. They are the few who have no fear when faced with danger. They are the ones who fight monsters, robots and the bad guys. They are Team Adventure Club!

***** END *****

About the Author

Joe Davison's work spans twenty-five years of writing, directing, and acting—and can be seen in the #1 Netflix hit *Stranger Things*...where he stars as Nerdy Tech in Season 2.

Joe Davison has also directed 6 feature films, including *Beauty is Skin Deep* (available on Amazon Prime) and the upcoming Major Motion Picture, *Sorority of the Damned.*

He is also a complete clown who loves nothing more than a bit of comedy and a good joke.

You can connect with me on:

- https://www.redgearsstudios.com
- https://twitter.com/Joeygigglepants
- https://www.facebook.com/joeygigglepants
- https://www.instagram.com/joeygigglepants

Also by Joe Davison

The Incredibly Not So True Adventures of Sam and William

Sam and William are known throughout the world as millionaire adventurists. They have journeyed to the far reaches of the planet. Their exploits have gained them riches and wealth beyond belief. But they have a higher calling, a majestic revere, a something or rather, a quest as it were, to save lives, even if they have to risk yours to do it. Time and time again, Sam and William have battled monsters, giant snakes, and even the undead. In the end they vow to keep each other alive, no matter who gets in the way.

Zoey saves Christmas

When Santa's puppy ends up under Zoey's Christmas tree, it's up to her, with the help of her best friend Brianna and her dad, his name's Andrew, to get the cute little fella back to the North Pole.

However, that's not as easy as it sounds when you have to keep the puppy from running away, win a snowball fight championship, and stop the meanest family anyone's ever met from stealing him... all just to keep the little guy safe.

Whew! It's a lot to manage when you're only nine years old.

Now everyone up at the North Pole is losing their minds trying to figure out what went wrong. Mort the elf blames himself, but to be fair, someone in the workshop did accidentally did break his glasses, and puppies can be pretty tricky.

Oh, yeah, and Mrs. Claus and the elves are trying to find the puppy with a helicopter and magic cookies.

If the puppy doesn't make it back to the North Pole before Santa returns, Santa won't get his present from Mrs. Claus!

Infinite chaos

A theological thriller about one man's destiny to fulfill an unseen prophecy; to stop the ultimate evil.

Death's campaign

This fantasy takes place in a different world. A strange and magical place built upon centuries of battle and bloodshed. Kingdom upon kingdom has fallen and been rebuilt on top of old skeletons of what were giant castles. Now at the turn of the new era the king of witches must first face his ultimate challenge. An evil sorcerer had assassinated his first born son on his birthday. Now King Febale, the powerful king of witches will go to any length to destroy the coward responsible for his son's death, but he will not go it alone. At his side is King Edwin: king of dragon's cave. Together the two kings along with their best warriors will scour the surrounding kingdoms to find the evil and end it for good. Follow as these two friends and kings march on in revenge as they alienate anything and anyone in their path as they storm the treacherous ice castle of Mt. Olefen and try to find peace in their time of mourning.

Shindy Shine

Shindy Shine is a compilation of poetry and short stories. A comprehensive exploration into the artistic avenue of the author's mind.

www.ingramcontent.com/pod-product-compliance
Ingram Content Group UK Ltd.
Pitfield, Milton Keynes, MK11 3LW, UK
UKHW022018190726
13853UKWH00005B/1993

9 798730 754706